THE SECRET INGREDIENT

ALSO BY STEWART LEWIS

You Have Seven Messages

THE SECRET INGREDIENT

Stewart Lewis

DELACORTE PRESS

Text copyright © 2013 by Stewart Lewis
Jacket photograph (girl) copyright © 2013 by Linda Brownlee

All rights reserved. Published in the United States by Delacorte Press, an imprint of Random House Children's Books, a division of Random House, Inc., New York.

Delacorte Press is a registered trademark and the colophon is a trademark of Random House, Inc.

Visit us on the Web! randomhouse.com/teens

Educators and librarians, for a variety of teaching tools, visit us at RHTeachersLibrarians.com

Library of Congress Cataloging-in-Publication Data
Lewis, Stewart.
The secret ingredient / Stewart Lewis. — First edition.
pages   cm
Summary: "After a chance meeting with a psychic, Olivia, a teen cook living in Los Angeles with her two dads and misfit brother, finds a vintage cookbook with handwritten notes inside and pieces together a story that turns a normal summer into a search for her birth mother"—Provided by publisher.
ISBN 978-0-385-74331-0 (hc) — ISBN 978-0-449-81001-9 (ebook)
[1. Self-realization—Fiction. 2. Mothers—Fiction. 3. Cooking—Fiction.
4. Los Angeles (Calif.)—Fiction.] I. Title.
PZ7.L5881Se 2013
[Fic]—dc23
2012027203

The text of this book is set in 11-point Sabon.
Book design by Trish Parcell

Printed in the United States of America

10 9 8 7 6 5 4 3 2 1

First Edition

for steve, my secret ingredient

Food is our common ground, a universal experience.
—*James Beard*

If you see a fork in the road, take it.
—*Yogi Berra*

CHAPTER 1

Every day is sunny in Los Angeles, but it's not exactly paradise. Yes, there are movie stars and palm trees, but there's also an area downtown called "skid row" where people live in a city of cardboard boxes, and it looks like some sort of war is going on. Bell, who is one of my dads, owns a restaurant, and sometimes we drive by skid row on our way to get the flowers that go on the tables. He named the restaurant FOOD, following the somewhat annoying trend of creating simple one-word names for places. It's sandwiched between a bookstore called Book and a coffee shop called Bean. A different approach might have been more interesting, like a Laundromat called Not Responsible for Lost Socks. There actually is a Laundromat near the restaurant, where I've been doing my whole family's laundry since I was eight. It doesn't have a sign, just a big brown triangle with a box of what looks like vintage detergent painted on it.

Bell's been letting me cook the special at FOOD every Saturday, and lately, as I've been expanding my palate and my menu, my dishes have become more popular. Some customers only come in on Saturday, and although Bell's definitely proud, and doesn't do much of the cooking anymore anyway, I think he's a little jealous of my success. The current chefs don't really mind—in fact, they get a kick out of it. One even asked me for my coleslaw recipe (shh, it's the jalapeño).

Bell has loved cooking his whole life, but he's been struggling with the restaurant for some time now. After the recession, people lost their taste for fine cuisine and, due to financial necessity or lingering prudence, are continuing to choose quantity over quality. The In-N-Out Burger on Sunset always looks like a rock concert, while you can hear crickets in the little boutique eateries. I'm not sure how bad the situation really is, but the other night I went into FOOD to prepare a marinade and it seemed like no one was there except the janitor. I realized I needed basil, so I headed for the walk-in cooler, opening the heavy silver door to find Bell crying on top of a crate of potatoes.

"Dad?"

"It's the onions," he said, both of us knowing that was a lie—the onions are prepped in the morning by the dishwashers. I took Bell's hand and walked him out of the cooler, sat him down at the chef's table, and poured him a glass of the cheap cabernet I was using for my marinade. I knew things were pretty bad, because even though he isn't rich by any means, Bell rarely drinks cheap wine. By his second sip I caught a hint of a grin. The thing about Bell is, he hardly ever says what he means, and I'm beginning to notice this pattern in other people as well. Everyone seems to have this duality about them: how they feel as opposed to what they're saying. Sometimes words are only clues—you have to put them together while reading the maps of people's faces. I'm pretty good at it when it comes to my family.

After he finished his wine, Bell stood up and held out his arms. I put down the lemon I was zesting and let him hug me, breathing in the musky scent of his cologne mixed with a hint of garlic—home.

"Are they going to take it all away?" I asked him.

He looked at me with his big brown eyes and shook his head, as if everything was fine, but I knew that was not the case. I had heard my dads fighting about the mortgage more than once, and I knew the bank people had come into the restaurant. For the first time in my life, I didn't know if Bell could make everything good again, if he could protect us from the world.

My name is Olivia, but everyone calls me by different nicknames. The only time anyone in my family uses my real name is when they're serious, or mad at me, which is not very often. I've always gotten good grades, and I'm not one of those teenagers who act out.

I'm sixteen going on seventeen, like the song. When I was little, Bell and I used to watch *The Sound of Music* all the time, and I always thought my mother, who gave me up when I was two days old, might have looked like Julie Andrews. I have reddish hair and blue eyes like her, but I'm definitely not an actress. Bell says I'm like a fine wine. If you want to get to know me the right way, you have to let me breathe first.

My older brother, Jeremy, is the opposite, very in-your-face. We're not blood related, but Bell adopted us from the same agency one year apart from each other. At the time, same-sex parents couldn't adopt as easily as they can today, but he got approved pretty quickly both times, as one of his former employees ran the agency. Bell moved in with Enrique, my other dad, soon after he adopted Jeremy. Enrique is not always the most reliable person, but he has many wonderful qualities. When you live in an imperfect, mismatched family like mine, you understand that love is about more than just blood. My dads raised me, took care of me when I was sick, taught me to walk, and read me to sleep every night. They are in my bones, a part of who I am. I can't imagine loving my birth parents any more.

Still, lately I've started to feel like something's missing. I've found myself wondering what would have happened if my mother hadn't given me up. It's hard to picture not being with my family, but it's easy to imagine myself in another life, in a more conventional household in the suburbs of some city where the lawns are manicured and I go on mother-daughter excursions with Julie Andrews. Bell always says we don't choose our family, and even if I had a choice, I'd choose Bell, Enrique, and Jeremy. But if I could change one thing, I would add a mother, even if only for short periods of time—someone who could, I don't know, take me to get my hair cut or something. Instead, the closest thing I've had to a mother is Enrique.

Even though he's technically a man, Enrique is very nurturing. When I was five, I stepped on a stingray at the public beach in Malibu, and it changed my life. I haven't been in the ocean since, and it sort of formed the person I was growing up: shy, a little different, and slightly removed in a city in which the ocean is such a big part of everyone's lives. Bell didn't seem to understand and took a passive approach to the Stingray Trauma, as it came to be called, but Enrique knew instinctively what I was going through and what to do: And not just because he grew up on the sea in Mexico and had a similar experience with a sand shark. From then on, whenever we went to the beach, Enrique would come up with all these elaborate games to play, none of which involved swimming. And he would take me to his friend's pool in the Hollywood Hills as a gateway to get me into the ocean again. It didn't work, but I did learn to swim well, and those afternoons in the pool with Enrique, nothing could touch me. Watching the valley below, sipping iced tea, floating on the inflatable rafts . . . I usually felt a little left of center, but being there with Enrique and the way he would look at me with pure, open love made me feel like the center of the world, which I guess is what mothers do.

I just finished my junior year at Silver Lake High. It's the first day of summer and, I hope, the day I finally get a job. In the past, I've waited tables for Bell, but business isn't exactly booming this year, so he doesn't need the extra help. I've been interviewing at different retail places, since I figure I should get something to put on my résumé that doesn't involve food, but I never seem to be a "good fit" for them. Maybe because my only work experience has been in Bell's restaurant. I have this feeling, though, that today is going to be different. Today, I have an interview that Enrique set up, at a casting agency his friend runs.

I get out of bed and walk over to the window. This morning my room has an orange glow to it. When the ball of red sun peeks over the horizon line east of our hill, it tends to wake me up—especially when I forget to shut my blinds. I slide the window open and hear the familiar sounds of birds and cars whizzing by in the distance, on the 101 freeway. A strange juxtaposition, but they seem to balance each other out. If someone asked me what L.A. sounds like, I would say birds and traffic.

I walk over to my dresser, slip on my vintage dress with the little blue flowers on it, and grab the champagne-colored sunglasses I bought at the Gas N Go for $3.99. They're a little indie rock for me, but I do look very Silver Lake, the area between Hollywood and downtown where we live. It's an offbeat, mostly Hispanic neighborhood that has a certain beauty, like a colorful but shabby real-life version of a montage from a hipster film. With the crazy mix of musicians, leather queens, yuppies, Mexicans, and bohemians (and some people who are all these in one), there's a feeling of acceptance. And Silver Lake is just known as being a *cool* place.

I go downstairs and find Enrique sleeping on the couch, which makes me a little uneasy. He was a dancer for the Mexico City Ballet, and his mangled feet are sticking out of the blanket. People think dancers are so elegant and graceful, and they are, but there's an underbelly to it all. He's had two operations on his knees, and his feet, well, let's just say they're not too pretty. I cover them up and quietly shuffle toward the kitchen.

I start to boil some water for eggs, and I feel my uneasiness begin to drift away with this familiar act. Poaching eggs is harder than you might think. The key is to put a little bit of vinegar in the water, to keep the egg from losing its shape. And I know it's a cliché, but this is a case in which timing is everything. I decide to also make what I call Red Is the New Black Potatoes. I take lots of fresh garlic and sauté it with extra-virgin olive oil. Then I slice some new red potatoes so thin they're just slivers. I fry them slowly until they're blackened at the edges. There's a fine line between blackened and burnt, and I know where that line is. It's all about texture. As far as I'm concerned, there's nothing worse than undercooked breakfast potatoes. You know, the watery, tasteless kind you get in a diner? *"Quelle horreur,"* Bell would say.

Enrique's phone rings, and I can't believe how quickly he gets it together, answering like he's been up for hours. I can tell it's a work call. He's a freelance stylist now, which means he buys clothes for actors. Sometimes I go with him, and he lets me pick out stuff too. The shows he's involved with are pretty low-budget, but once he worked on a movie that was shot in Hawaii and starred Demi Moore. We all thought his career would take off after that, but he just went back to doing bad reality shows and working with his soap opera clients, living paycheck to paycheck. If you ask me, I'd say Enrique was in his prime when he was dancing all over the world. Being a stylist is just something he ended up doing. He doesn't even like nice clothes for himself—he basically wears khakis and polo shirts, which seems like an obvious play to defy stereotypes. His name is Enrique, not Biff, and even though he looks the part, he will never go sailing in Nantucket.

He comes into the kitchen and picks at my potatoes.

"Ollie, these are dreamy-like."

"Thanks, Papá."

Even though Enrique has been in America for almost twenty years, he still has his own way of speaking. Most people find it charming, but Bell tends to correct him.

I place my poached eggs on seven-grain toast, garnish them with fresh Pecorino, sprinkle some rosemary on my potatoes, and sit down by the kitchen window. Every time I finish cooking a dish, I feel this swell in my chest when I look at the finished product, at this thing that I've created. We skimp on everything in our house except food; I need my supplies if I'm going to do what I do best. Enrique makes a smoothie, pours us each a glass, and joins me. A few minutes later, Bell comes in and goes straight for the coffeemaker. His hair seems to be living in a different area code than his head. Thick and wavy, it has a little gray in it, but Enrique says it's one of Bell's best physical qualities, and he always has his hands in it, though not as much recently. Bell doesn't look at either of us and just says, "Monday, Monday."

I need a job, not just to help out with money, but because, as much as I love our little house, it can also feel like the walls are closing in, especially when my dads are acting distant toward each other. And now that Jeremy has moved out, I have no one to roll my eyes with.

Jeremy is eighteen and thinks he's going to be a rock star. He's been playing gigs since he was fifteen, basically anywhere they'll book him. He's roommates with his drummer, a janitor named Phil who Bell calls "a real winner." Neither of our dads were too happy when Jeremy announced that he was deferring college for a year to try and get a record deal, but they're doing their best to be supportive. Jeremy practices all the time, and his latest demo is actually pretty good. He also had a decent crowd the last time he played at Silver Lake Lounge.

Bell kisses my head, then heads out to the restaurant. I

asked Enrique not to tell him about the interview in case it doesn't work out, so he doesn't know to wish me luck. Enrique is running out too and gives me a secret thumbs-up sign and mouths "Go for it."

I finish my breakfast and leave my dish in the sink. One thing I don't like about cooking is doing dishes. But the great thing is if you cook for someone, they will most likely beg to do the dishes for you. And although Enrique always leaves dried toothpaste in the sink and his polo shirts draped over all the chairs, he loves my cooking and is pretty good at "washing up," as my best friend, Lola, would say. Lola's from England and knows a lot more about the world than I do. I'm meeting her for coffee before my interview to take my mind off it.

Before I leave, I go to my room and switch to my black sunglasses. If I'm going to get a job, I need to look a little older and exude confidence. I look in the mirror, trying to see a different side of myself. When I was little I didn't talk much, but one day in third grade, when we got to make cinnamon rolls with the sixth graders in home ec, my teacher told my dads I wouldn't shut up. That was when Bell started cooking at home with me. The next day we made pastries from scratch, and for the first time, something clicked, and I became fascinated by how incredible it is to make something from practically nothing. I realized that almost everything starts in a bowl, with flour and eggs—it begins with the human hand. My whole outlook on food changed. Ever since then, cooking has felt like the most natural thing. It's also a way to get out of my head for a while. Some people find it tedious, but for me, it's an escape. Plus, when I see someone's eyes slowly shut in bliss after a bite of something I made, it makes me feel like I can do anything.

CHAPTER 2

Our street is called Maltman Avenue, and it's so steep it could be in San Francisco. The houses are painted colors like butter-yellow, sky-blue, and burnt orange, and there are always kids playing and barbecues going, international spices hovering in the air. Our house is a two-bedroom bungalow, which is another name for "very small house." But we do have a garage, where Jeremy lived through most of high school, practicing his electric guitar and drinking too much Red Bull. Before that, we shared a room, which was beyond cramped. Being in junior high and sharing a room with my brother was pretty much a nightmare, but we somehow got through it.

At the bottom of our street is the eastern part of Sunset Boulevard, not the famous part with the shiny billboards and tourist traps. There's the 99-cent store, a Korean tailor, and a place called Mack Video (which Bell calls Crack Video because of the sketchy people who congregate in the parking lot next to it). I pass the trendy new Indian restaurant and several retro-themed cafes and vintage clothing stores that seem to have popped up in the last few months.

I meet Lola at the coffee shop on Sunset and Fountain, and before I have a chance to sit down, she starts filling me in on her current crush, the Asian kid who works at the taco place.

"Duality," I say, kind of under my breath.

"What are you on about, Livie?"

Lola grew up in London but has lived here since she was twelve. I love having a British best friend. It makes me feel intercontinental even though I've never left California.

"I've just been noticing duality in everything lately."

"Well," she says, wiping her upper lip, "as you should."

Lola's mother runs a yoga studio in Atwater Village, and her dad is a documentary producer for the BBC. She always has way more money than I do and pays for everything. It sometimes makes me uncomfortable, but she's not the type to hold it against me. Apparently, her father still gets his salary in British pounds, which go way farther than the dollar. Especially when you're buying fish tacos, which we do on a regular basis, not only because we like them, but because they are served by her crush, a guy named Jin.

"So what is it about him, anyway?" I ask her.

"He just seems like he could clean up well, you know? Put him in a dinner jacket, and he might just hit the mark."

"Lola, he's like, fifteen."

"A girl can dream."

I smile, thinking of Jin serving tacos in a suit.

"And I know it's a bit of a stereotype," Lola says, "but he seems very intelligent, you know? Like he's solving math theorems on his breaks from . . . tortilla rolling or what have you."

"Kneading."

"Right. Well, what you 'knead,' darling, is a job."

So much for keeping my mind off my interview.

"Yeah. I saw an ad for a babysitter—"

"No offense, Livie, but you're a bit on the mellow side for that, don't you think?"

"Well, it doesn't matter anyway. When I called, they said they wanted someone who had experience with children. But actually, I have a lead on something way better. Papá set up an interview for me with a casting agent who needs an assistant."

"Now we're getting warmer. You're always on about nuance. You'll need that for casting, don't you reckon?"

This is why I love Lola. She always seems to say the right thing. And even when she doesn't, it still sounds great in her accent. I pull out the address Enrique gave me and look at my watch. "I'd better get going, the interview's at eleven."

"Right. Why don't you come by the studio after? I'll be taking roll for all the pudgy ladies at Mum-yoga. We can go get tacos!"

I try to leave some money for my chai, but Lola waves my hand away.

"Okay, we can get tacos only if you let me buy them," I say.

"We'll just see about that. Good luck, Livie!"

She kisses me on each cheek as we get up to go, then leaves in a flourish, her scarf trailing behind her. Lola is glamorous, funny, and so naturally beautiful that some people find her intimidating. I've had a fair amount of friends growing up, but she's the first person who really got me. When she transferred to my school two years ago, all the popular girls wanted to become her friend because she's British. But she didn't really care for them. It's almost like she has this X-ray vision that can see through fakeness. We became lab partners in science, and when I named our frog Toast, she took a shine to me. I invited her over after school and taught her how to make oatmeal cookies from scratch. I added dried cranberries, which she thought was the coolest thing ever. Even though it's only been two years, I can't imagine my life without Lola in it. It's like I used to live in black-and-white, and when Lola came along everything was suddenly in color.

*　*　*

Walking up Sunset toward Vermont Avenue, I pass a random schizophrenic discreetly talking to himself, a Hispanic family, and a couple of twentysomething dudes with guitars on their backs. When I get to the building, I realize it's the tallest one for miles.

The lobby is shiny and stark, with hard sofas that look more like warped benches. I slip my sunglasses onto the top of my head and step into a huge elevator with white walls and a metal ceiling, and press 17. It stops at the twelfth floor, and a woman is revealed, as if the automatic doors were theater curtains dramatically drawn. She's probably early forties, draped in loose-fitting, earth-toned clothes. She has a clear complexion and alert eyes. There's a streak of gray in her otherwise black hair. She clutches a small leather bag.

"Going down?" she asks.

"No, up to seventeen."

She draws a circle in the air with her finger, as if calculating the journey, and says, "Oh well, I'll take the scenic route."

The doors close with her inside, and I can immediately smell her. Cloves and lemon. As we ascend, I notice her perfect posture. She stands so straight you can almost imagine a wire pulled taut from the bottom of her spine to the crown of her head. Lola's mother has it too. She does yoga every day and only eats blueberries for breakfast. I usually don't talk to strangers, so I'm surprised to hear myself say, "Do you do yoga?"

Before she can answer, the elevator stops abruptly. After a few seconds, we both realize we're not on a floor.

"I believe the word is *practice*, but yes," she answers sweetly.

I look around the elevator stupidly, like there's a trapdoor or something. The woman is very calm, as if this sort of thing happens all the time. We decide to wait a minute or two before pressing the emergency call button.

"Maybe it'll just start up again," I say, trying to be positive.

The woman pulls out some grapes and offers me one. I take it to be polite, but then realize it has seeds—awkward. She notices my discomfort and says, "You can just crunch and swallow them, like a nut. They actually have more nutrients than the grape itself."

A grape doesn't have a self, I think. But instead I say, "Good to know," and stare at the red button.

The woman steps closer and puts her clear eyes on me acutely, and suddenly I feel exposed. Since we're trapped, I can't really claim personal space.

"I was only stuck in an elevator one other time," she says, crunching on a grape seed, "and believe it or not, it was with the queen of England."

Yeah, right.

"Really?"

"Yes. I was hired by her estate manager to do some channeling work."

There are a lot of bohemian types in Silver Lake, and

I've heard about channeling—basically when people summon spirits of others who then speak through them—but it still seems a little far-fetched to me.

"You're a . . . channeler?"

She gives me a look so sharp I wouldn't be surprised if darts start shooting out of her pupils. I move out of her way just in case.

"I like to say visionary. I do psychic work, but I also do guided meditation and past-life integration. I get called to consult with, well, powerful people."

I think of Enrique and what he's always saying about the class system. "So the fact that you're a psychic for people with money makes it more credible?"

I can't believe I've said something so rude. I reach out to push the red button, but before I can, she grabs my wrist, not too tight, but enough to make me tremble a little.

"Hang on a minute," she says.

I wonder if this is some sort of setup, if she knew we'd be here all along. I try to remain calm and wait. She looks at me like she's examining a lab rat, and I can feel my forehead getting moist. Then she says something that makes everything else disappear.

"I know what it's like not having a mother."

I feel a dropping sensation in my stomach, and a tightening in my throat. "What?"

I slowly back up until I reach the elevator wall and sit down. Even though I'm freaking out, I can almost hear

Bell laughing. He's never bought into the whole New Age thing.

"How did you know that?"

"It's what I do," she replies evenly.

I decide to test her.

"Okay, how come I don't have a mother?"

A look of pity colors her face, as if my test is too easy.

"She gave you up for adoption."

I stare at her and realize my jaw is slack.

"Um, this is getting a little creepy," I say. "Can we press the button now?"

She sits down directly across from me. I do my best to remain calm.

"I'll tell you what," she says, arranging herself into a cross-legged position. "While we're here, why don't you let me read you?"

"Look, I don't believe—"

She holds up her hands. "Take what you want from it. I usually get thousands of dollars for this, and I'm offering—"

"No, it's okay, really."

"No charge."

Her gaze softens a little, and I think she's going to smile, but suddenly her expression goes blank. "You have an older brother. There's fire in him."

I can feel my heart banging on the wall of my chest. I try to think of Bell, who would still be laughing at this point. Or would he?

"He will soar."

I put my head in my hands and pretend this isn't happening. But when I look up and see her pure, honest expression, something tells me to trust her.

"Okay, just do it."

She studies my palms, writes down my birth date in a little notebook she has, tells me to stick out my tongue (I laugh a little during that part) and look her in the eye for as long as I can. I last several minutes, then lower my gaze to my sneakers. She takes my hand and holds it gently.

"This summer."

"What?"

"Last summer there were some changes for you?"

I think of Jeremy moving out, and my breasts suddenly appearing.

"Yes."

"This summer will be different—pivotal." I try to smile at her to lighten things up, but nothing seems to crack her concentration. She becomes visibly emotional, like she's holding back tears. "You must be aware of your choices. I know you're young, but you're an old soul. Please remember—all your choices are connected."

A single tear falls from her left eye and makes a tiny splat on the elevator floor. For some reason I think of William Hurt's fake tear in *Broadcast News*. Bell's always quoting the old movies we watch together, and he does a pretty good Holly Hunter.

"Yours is a delicate spirit, but it will get stronger, and

fast. I see your roots taking hold. You will have guidance from someone in the past. I also see a young man. And I'm not sure why, but food is important somehow."

She stares at me for what seems like an hour, then finally pushes the button and goes back into stranger mode. As we wait for the maintenance guy to radio in, she barely looks at me, until the elevator finally starts to move and we reach the casting agent's floor.

"Do you have a card?" I ask.

She lets out a quick, hearty laugh and says, "If you need me, I will be there."

"Okay, well, thanks," I say, but it comes out as more of a question.

CHAPTER 3

The door to the casting agency is metallic silver and says J. TUCKER CASTING in dark red letters. I stare at my reflection in the door, wondering if opening it will really be of any significance. Is it true that every decision we make is connected and is a catalyst to a string of reactions in the universe? Like a caterpillar becomes a butterfly in Japan and then a baby cries in Russia, and a dog dies in Spain? I open the door slowly, telling myself to "just chill," as Jeremy would say.

To my left, there are two skinny girls in miniskirts sitting on plastic chairs and looking nervous and twitchy, eyeing me as possible competition for whatever they're auditioning for. It must be so belittling, the whole auditioning thing.

When I was fifteen there was a photographer friend of Enrique's who tried to get me to model, who said with the contrast of my red hair and blue eyes that I had a real shot. But when I got the pictures taken I was so anxious it caused me to sweat under the lights, and the photos came out pretty lame. I remember bringing them home to my dads, who said they were "wonderful," which was code for "awkward." I told them that I no longer wanted to be a model, and they accepted it with a hint of relief. I smile at the girls, thinking of that experience and how grateful I am to be beyond it.

There's a reception desk that is unmanned, which must be for the job that needs to be filled. A woman in a sports coat, jeans, and loafers comes out of an office door behind the desk. She's one of those beautiful tomboy types who could totally change her look by letting her hair down and taking off the sports coat, which actually works for her. Her glasses have jewels embedded in the sides, and her thin lips settle into a smirk, which seems like their default position.

She looks about thirty, maybe younger, but you can never really tell in Los Angeles, where some people think Botox is a necessity, like getting your teeth cleaned. Speaking of, her teeth are so white I may need to put my sunglasses back on to fight the glare.

She addresses the girls first, holding up her hand, then turns to me and says, "Can I help you?"

"Yes, hi, I'm Olivia. I'm here about the job?"

She lets out a quick laugh, and I realize hundreds of people come in here all the time for "jobs," so I specify. "Enrique got me in touch with your office. You're Janice Tucker?"

"Oh! Yes, you're Enrique's daughter, right?"

I nod.

"Great, why don't you sit down. I'll be right with you."

During the next twenty minutes, the two girls are called in to Janice's office to read what they call "sides," which I gather are basically the lines the actors have to read. The walls are so thin I can hear everything. One side is a commercial, and the other is a dramatic monologue in which the girl is about to run away and is saying goodbye to her dog. Her speech is supposed to be truthful and deep because she's talking to her dog. It's written so poorly that it's almost good.

When the last girl leaves, Janice actually says, "I'll call you," and then turns to me with a big smile.

Strangely enough, I bet Janice Tucker is her real name. As one of many steps in their plan to be bigger than themselves, everyone in Hollywood uses fake names. Part of the illusion of fame, I guess. Out of character for L.A., J. Tucker Casting has an authenticity to it, and so does Janice's straightforward demeanor. I bet she could host a dinner party *and* gut the fish beforehand. She seems tough but kind—like you could tell her secrets and know they were safe, but she'd be honest about what she thought of you.

Janice motions me inside her office, where I sit in the same chair as the hundreds of actors and actresses who have come through this door.

"How are you?" she asks.

"Relieved that I won't be confessing to a dog," I say.

Janice dabs some antibacterial liquid into her hands and chuckles as she rubs them together.

"I know, it's a Lifetime movie. They're horribly written but strangely addictive once you start watching them. Olivia, right?"

"Yes, but you can call me . . . whatever."

During the next five minutes, Janice's phone rings seven times, and we have a choppy conversation about the job. I tell her I have "assisted" Enrique, which is, to say the least, an embellishment. I also tell her that I cook a weekly special at FOOD, which seems irrelevant but feels good to say. Even though I sense that we have a strange connection, the whole process is a bit random and rushed, which is why I'm somewhat surprised when she puts down the phone and says, "Listen, I'm in a bind here. My former assistant took off yesterday for India to go to a . . . meditation school or something. So, how about tomorrow at ten? Can you start then?"

"Yes."

It was that easy? I didn't even ask her how much she's paying. I'm just so happy I have a job.

"Dress business casual, and bring a photo ID."

"Great, thanks . . ."

She senses my hesitation and says, "Call me Janice."

"Thanks, Janice."

I realize I'm blushing as I head toward the door. As I press down the handle, again I hear her steady voice.

"Oh, and Red?"

I turn around, and her smirk is slightly more pronounced.

"No sneakers."

I nod, looking down at my Chuck Taylors. *Whoops.*

The faint smell of the psychic woman is still in the elevator when I get back in. During the swift ride down, I can't help but think she's right. Maybe J. Tucker Casting *is* a door to something bigger than I could know. Maybe right now a bird is flying for the first time, a forest is burning down, a storm is wiping out a village. Maybe a seed is being planted in rich soil by an old wrinkled hand, a key is being dropped into a deep lake, and my life will be forever different. I try to feel it. The moment that changes everything.

CHAPTER 4

When I get to the yoga studio, a class is already in session. Lola is at the front desk listening to her iPod and flipping through an *L.A. Weekly*. When she notices me, she shuts the paper dramatically, comes around, and gives me a huge hug.

"You got the job!"

She can tell from my smile. They say that best friends finish each other's sentences. With Lola, sometimes we don't even have to speak at all.

"Tops!"—British for "Great!"—"How much does it pay?"

"I forgot to ask. I start tomorrow. What's business casual?"

When it comes to fashion, Lola's the expert. I really don't put too much effort into my clothes. I've never understood why girls in my school are so obsessed with designer jeans and "accessorizing." I find most of my clothes at Out of the Closet, a secondhand store that benefits AIDS research. I got teased a lot when I was in seventh and eighth grades for my thrifty look, but then of course vintage became cool, so I guess you could say I was ahead of the curve. It sounds weird, but sometimes when I buy used clothing, I imagine who the previous owner was, where she liked to eat and travel. Every day, I'm carrying the history of other girls and women on my back. I like the idea of being a walking patchwork of other people's lives.

"Don't worry," Lola says, "we'll get you sorted. Let's get out of here. I'm taking you to the mall."

As Lola weaves her Mini Cooper through Hollywood to the Beverly Center, I tell her about the psychic woman in the elevator.

"It's not *like* you to pay any mind to someone like that, Livie!" Lola sounds incredulous.

"I know, but—it felt like she knew me. The first thing she said to me was 'I know what it's like not having a mother.' And this morning I had this feeling that today was going to be different. I thought it was just about the job, but maybe it's more."

This makes Lola think.

"That *is* a bit odd. But roots, a past, a boy? That's all

fairly standard stuff. And food's important to everyone—although admittedly more to you."

"I don't know, there's a lot going on right now, you know? Jeremy's floundering, and my dads seem stressed. . . . I think they're basically on the verge of losing the restaurant. It would just be nice to think that maybe . . ."

"Livie, you concentrate too much on others. I know it's your family and all, but you have to sort yourself out. It's time. You do the laundry for your whole family! Not to mention cook for them. I know you love that, but the truth is, you give a bit too much. I used to be the same way, but lately I've stopped worrying about my totally dysfunctional family and am just trying to work on myself."

"I know. How's the art class?"

Lola has a thing for art, and always takes me around to museums, although I never understand it the way she does. Lately she's been taking art classes, but it might be just another one of her temporary projects. Last month it was volunteering at a homeless shelter, which lasted two whole days.

"The teacher's a bit weird, but I like working with oil. I'm making a piece for Jin. It's got some Japanese letters in it."

"But he's Korean."

"Same continent."

Lola takes the ticket at the parking garage and winds the car too fast up the circular ramp. By the time she parks, I feel queasy. She grabs her purse, flips her hair, and says in an American accent, "Okay, girl, let's get you business casual!"

Malls make me nervous, but aside from when she's driving, being with Lola puts me at ease. She chooses two outfits for me. It feels weird wearing new clothes with the tags still on them, but maybe it *is* time for a change, for me to focus on my own life rather than everyone else's. And with me making my own money, I'll be able to afford it. Lola plops down her credit card, and I promise to pay her back with my first paycheck.

As we walk over to Banana Republic, Lola keeps talking about Jin. Then, out of the blue, she asks me if I still haven't heard from Dish Boy. She means Theo.

Last summer when I first started cooking at FOOD, Theo got hired as a dishwasher. He was saving up for a racing bike, and he taped a picture of it over the sink. One afternoon I was flipping through a magazine and saw a black-and-white picture of a windy road with a leafless tree at the end of it. I taped it next to the picture of his bike, and he smiled at me in a way I had never seen before. His smile said: *I'd like to get to know you.*

I had kissed a few boys, but I never really liked any of them that way. Theo had jet-black hair, and his bottle-green eyes easily upstaged the lightly scattered acne on his face.

One day, after weeks of shy flirting, he asked me out on a date. He was really nervous, and kept staring down at his feet. He told me to meet him at the 99-cent store the next night. Something came over me, like a wash of light. I felt beautiful, and very alive. I debated what to wear for hours, which I had never really done before. I put on mascara and lip gloss. I dabbed a little vanilla extract behind my ears.

Theo never showed up. I waited for over an hour. And the next day, he didn't come into work. Bell didn't have a home number for him, and he wasn't picking up his cell. That was it; he just vanished.

I know it seems like it shouldn't have affected me so much. I'd known Theo for less than a month. But he was the first boy I ever thought I could really like . . . maybe even love. It took me months and months of wondering why, what, and how, until I finally let it go. Well, more like buried it deep inside me, because when Lola says the words *Dish Boy*, my breath shortens, and I have to sit down in the little faux living room set up in the back of Banana Republic. She knew what a nightmare it was for me, so I'm wondering why she's even bringing it up.

"No," I say.

"Oh. I was just thinking about the 'young man' part of the psychic's 'prediction,' you know? Regardless, we'll have to get you on the market, Livie," she says, holding a frilly white top in front of me. Lola has tons of advice about boys, but I've never actually seen her date anyone.

Back in Silver Lake, we pass by a bunch of kids in an alley, and I recognize Jeremy and his drummer, Phil. They're lighting fireworks. When we were little, Jeremy used to protect me. One time these Mexican kids were teasing me

31

about having two dads, and he slashed the tires on their bikes. He ended up getting beaten up pretty badly, but that's the way Jeremy is. He takes dares and rushes head-first into things, and I have a feeling his wounds make him feel alive.

For as long as I could use a knife, I've made Jeremy gazpacho, his favorite thing to eat, and it makes sense. It's more of an angry dish, especially the way I make it. The chili pepper element isn't exactly subtle. When Lola and I get home, I decide to make him a batch, maybe because I'm feeling a little frustrated that Lola brought up Theo. It's simple to make, but it requires a lot of labor, and chopping always calms me down. The tomatoes are from our neighbor Davida's garden. She's a former Broadway actress who is now a "life coach," among other things. Is that the dumbest phrase ever? Life is not something that can be mastered by some strength training or through a miraculous goal in overtime. It's more like learning through experience.

Lola is already trying the gazpacho before I add the fresh lemon juice and cilantro. She calls it "divine," which is pretty much her highest compliment. I tell her she always eats my dishes before they're done.

"That's the best bit! You have to taste the process."

I love how she says "*pro*-cess." I smile and start to chop the cilantro, also from Davida's garden. In exchange for Davida giving us produce, I walk her big chocolate Lab named Hank. If there's anything on the planet that em-

bodies love, it's that dog. He loves everyone uncondi-
tionally, even the mean guy at the video store. I've been
walking him for six years, so a lot of people think he's my
dog. Sometimes at night I can hear Davida singing to him.
It might sound weird, but it's not if you know Davida.

Lola has to run and pick up her "auntie" from the air-
port, and when she leaves I put on KCRW. It's a college
station that plays a lot of cool stuff. As a matter of fact,
they were the first station to play Coldplay when they
were nobodies. One time Jeremy went to the station with
his guitar and camped outside their offices until someone finally let him in and actually allowed him to play a
little. The guy said he was talented but didn't have the
right songs. This is the feedback Jeremy has been getting
for years. Right now the station's playing someone named
M. Ward. He sounds groggy, and the music is a little
creepy, but it has a soothing effect. I zone out until Davida's big head appears in the window behind the sink.

"What's wrong, Chef? I know that look."

"Well, I met a psychic."

"Oh." She seems skeptical. When she offered to "coach"
me in the past, I wanted none of it. Now she probably
thinks a phony tricked me.

"Come in, try some gazpacho."

Davida is wearing her usual mix of sweats and loose
bohemian clothes. She tries the gazpacho, and her eye-
lids slowly close, the first sign I've done a good job. I tell
her about the elevator woman. The more I talk, the more

intrigued she is. She takes another bite and says, "Yummers." Her dorky word choice would embarrass me if she were my mother, but with Davida it somehow works.

"Thanks."

"Listen, Chef, she may be on to something."

"I don't know. I do feel like something is happening, or about to happen. Or maybe I'm just gullible."

"If there's one thing you're not, it's gullible. By the way," Davida says as she steps toward the door, "how's that brother of yours?"

"I'm about to find out."

"Well, tell him I said hi." Then she's gone.

I fill a large Tupperware bowl with my freshly made gazpacho and head over to Jeremy's place. It's about four stops on the bus, and two skater kids sitting across from me stare at my big bowl like they haven't eaten in weeks. Or maybe they have the munchies. I cover it a little with my arm and count the palm trees out the window. There are twelve between our two bus stops. I've used palm trees to measure distance for as long as I can remember. That's one thing I can always count on. I may not have a mother, a boyfriend, or a brother who stays out of trouble, but the palm trees will always stand tall and strong for me—mile markers of my city, and sturdy beacons of survival.

CHAPTER 5

My brother's apartment has steep, faded green steps that lead to a dull brown building split into two small units. At first it seems like it's going to be a cute place, but then reality sets in. I think they each pay two hundred dollars a month. I don't really know where Jeremy gets his share of the rent, but I know it's not from Bell. Enrique, on the other hand, has been known to secretly fund Jeremy's "pipe dream," as Bell calls it.

The window is open, so I peek in. Jeremy's recording on the vintage four-track recorder he got at a garage sale in Echo Park. He claims it once belonged to Elliott Smith. The song he's doing has a catchy hook, like something old and new at the same time. It's the type of song I could actually imagine hearing on the radio. He sings into the microphone that Bell got him for his eighteenth birthday.

"There's a hole in the sky
And there's acid in the air
Toxic waste in the sea
And there's dirt on our hands
And blood at our feet
Whatcha doin' there, people?
Whatcha doin' there, people?
Destroyin' the world."

He hits a bum chord on his guitar and yells, "Damn!"

I take the opportunity to knock. He opens the door and smiles.

"Hey, Ol, what's going on?"

"Brought you some gazpacho."

"No way, you rock. I'm starving. I've been eating day-old bagels for three days."

I give him a look. "So technically they're three-day-old bagels. Sounds starchy," I say.

He grabs a big used spoon that's lying on the coffee table and digs in. He takes a couple bites while playing back the track. Over the music, he says, "Dude, you have to like, mass produce this or something."

Jeremy is the only person who can call me dude without it feeling weird.

He turns the track down a little. "What's the secret?"

When we were little, before Bell had his own restaurant, he used to manage a place that had some underground success. The cook was this guy named Eli, who would always squeeze my cheeks. I would stand there, mesmerized by how he cut his onions, waiting for him to slice off a finger. He told me that with every dish I make, there should be a secret ingredient, something that comes from that chef alone, like a handprint. Something that completes the dish and makes it unique.

I smile and say to Jeremy, "If you must know . . . honey."

"Wow. Can I just get an IV of this next to my bed?"

"Then you wouldn't be able to taste it, dummy."

Jeremy smiles like he knew that already. I tell him I like the song, but it's a little depressing.

"Listen, Ol, people don't want shiny happy songs. The world is in chaos. Recession, unemployment, wars, natural disasters. I want to write songs that speak to that, you know? Sweet but spicy, like your soup. It's like, this deal I was offered, some slick guy with big offices on Melrose wants me to record a demo, but not of my songs. I met the songwriter, she seemed cool enough, but the songs? Ol, they're like watered-down carbon copies of the lame-ass crap on the charts. I turned it down. I just gotta get someone to believe in what I have to say, you know what I mean, dude? As an artist."

"Well, sometimes you have to sell out a little to be able to make your voice heard." I have no idea what I'm talking about, but it sounds kind of right.

"Yeah, well, she's definitely hot."

I see Jeremy has her website up on his laptop. She's sitting by a piano wearing a tank top.

"Jeremy! What is she, like, thirty?"

"Probably. I just can't deal with these emotionally adolescent chicks. I need a forward thinker." He finishes the gazpacho and licks his lips, my reminder of a job well done.

"Anyway, do you know what's going on with the restaurant?" I ask, changing the subject.

"It's not good," Jeremy says. "I went home to get some stuff and the Dads were freaking."

For as long as I can remember, Jeremy has called Bell and Enrique "the Dads" whenever he's referring to both of them. Like me, he calls Bell "Dad" and Enrique "Papá," which is what Enrique used to call his own dad in Mexico.

"I guess they have to come up with four large by the end of the month. And that'll only buy them another month."

"I knew it was bad, but not that bad," I tell him.

"Dad was cleaning out the air vents and the closets."

Whenever Bell has something going on, he cleans like a maniac. It's kind of like me with cooking. I guess it balances out whatever mess is in our lives. When Bell told his parents he was gay, they basically disowned him, which is so lame. I was ten, and I came home to find him cleaning the refrigerator. Even at that age, I could tell something was wrong. He had just been to Washington to try to see his parents, and his mother had slammed the door in his face. Can you imagine? When he finished, I helped him put all the food back in. Then we made date bars, because it seemed like cooking was the logical thing to do. While we waited for them to bake, he told me about his parents. How his father used to drag him to baseball games, and how his mother used to sing him to sleep. The way he talked about them, with such love in his eyes, made me super sad. I told him that they were his parents, and that they would come around. But they never did. Here we are almost seven years later, and I've still never met them.

Jeremy gets up and starts to pace, and I can sense a rant inside him that's about to be released.

"They don't know I heard, but listen, sis, we gotta help them. I'm gonna take the money I got for my electric and try to buy an ice cream truck. You know some of those guys pull in like five hundred bucks a day? Crazy. Hardly any overhead except the van. Phil's friend has one for sale. It needs fixing, but I got this mechanic guy who'll do it if I give his son guitar lessons. I'm trying to get it running by Friday. Won't have a license, but half the trucks don't anyway."

Suddenly my little job feels inadequate. I know his plan is a tad haphazard, but I'm surprised he's so on top of it. Of course he loves Bell, but he's usually too wrapped up in his own world to see anything else.

"Well, I got a job today," I announce.

"No way! *¿Dónde?*"

"A casting agency."

Jeremy kind of half smiles and half frowns and says, "Whatever works." He's not a fan of agents in general.

"So between the two of us we should be able to really help."

"Perfect." Jeremy gets quiet and looks around his dilapidated living room. There's a dorm fridge with what looks like old yogurt spilled down the side of it, and a dusty TV with a makeshift aluminum foil antenna. "I'm young, you know? I can deal with living like this. But the Dads, I don't think they can handle this setback. Not now."

"I know."

I decide to leave Jeremy to record the rest of his song. On my way out, he grabs my shoulder and turns me around. "Listen, don't tell them about my plan."

"I won't. Bell doesn't know about my job yet, either."

Jeremy tousles my hair like he always does and goes for his guitar. As I leave, I feel uplifted by his concern. I know that if we're actually going to get through this, it will have to be as a team.

When I get back home I see Enrique going through bills, and his face looks sullen.

"Papá, you want some avocado toast?"

He nods and smiles at me briefly. He's always been obsessed with avocados. His best friend from ballet, a short woman named Luisa, got him on the kick. Apparently avocados are all she ate. He usually eats them right out of the skin with a spoon, but I've tried to find different ways to serve them. In omelets, with tuna, and most recently on seven-grain toast with lemon juice and chili flakes. Making it this way is more daring, the spice giving it an edge. Avocado has a soothing texture, but the chili flakes counteract it. As the bread is toasting I peek through the kitchen door. Enrique has sharp cheekbones, smooth skin, and soft brown eyes. Most of the time, he has a sort of pleasant, satisfied look on his face, but sometimes his features distort to look totally different—not ugly, but almost. He has that look now.

When I bring Enrique the avocado toast he looks up at me and smiles again, his eyes a little moist at the corners. He takes a bite and moans, a good sign. There's a reason people bring food to houses when someone has died. Food brings people together and gives you a comfort that nothing else can. It's more than nourishment, although that's a big part. When our taste buds come alive, other things seem possible. Hope, change, a new outlook on things. Especially when it's the right dish.

"Do you believe all our choices are connected?" I ask him.

"Well, yes and no."

"I feel like things are happening beyond me, bigger than me; some plan is starting to unfold. I felt it this morning, even before . . ."

He smiles again, which I'm glad to see.

"Of course it is, Ollie, and for you, the sky is the top."

"The limit," I say. "Speaking of limits, I know about the restaurant. What's really going on?"

"How was Janice?" he asks, clearly having forgotten about the interview until now. Or maybe he was waiting until we were talking about something he wanted to avoid. "She texted me that she hired you. Congratulations!"

"Yeah. She seems really great. But you didn't answer my question."

"It's more than the restaurant, Ollie."

"What?"

Enrique's phone buzzes, and he puts down the avocado toast and starts checking his texts.

I ask him again what he meant, but he just waves his hand, casually but as graceful as a ballet movement. I take his plate and eat the last bite while heading back into the kitchen.

Before I get into bed I lay out clothes for my first day at work. When I was little, Enrique would do this for me. He would sneak things onto my outfits that would balance them out—make them seem special even though they were secondhand. His grandmother's silk scarf. A belt that Luisa gave him to give me. I knew these things didn't really change the fact that my clothes were used, but the gesture always touched my heart.

As I try to fall asleep, I picture myself walking through the door to J. Tucker Casting and wonder once again if the psychic woman really knew what she was talking about. Part of me hopes so. A lot of my life has felt like a preparation for something bigger, like I've been waiting on a platform for a train to take me somewhere I've never been but will recognize when I get there. I think about the chef with his secret ingredient, and I wonder if I'll ever stop feeling that something is missing—if I'll find *my* secret ingredient.

CHAPTER 6

The morning sun fills our kitchen with elongated rectangles of light. When I was a toddler, I used to hop in and out of them, imagining that the light held special powers that were transferred to me as I stood inside their warmth. To this day, they still seem like magic to me. I start to slice some melon when I hear the signature squeak of the screen door. It's Davida, with a very excited Hank on a leash. I think he can smell the ripe melon. I forgot it's Thursday, one of the days I walk him. I look at the clock. I have time before I need to head to work.

"Sorry to drop and dash," Davida says, "but I've got a meeting in Santa Monica, and I slept right through my alarm. Haven't done that in years!"

I take Hank from her, feeding him a piece of melon, which he swallows whole.

44

"No problem. Good luck!" I give her a reassuring smile.

"Thanks, Chef, you're a lifesaver. See you later."

She's off, and it's just Hank and me. I scratch his ears and he licks my cheek. I grab a plastic bag and step outside. The sun shines 340 days a year in L.A., so when it's cloudy or rainy, people get really depressed and don't leave their houses. I enjoy the rain, because sometimes, like today, L.A. feels like a movie set where every morning someone turns on the sun and paints the sky blue. Rain makes it more real.

I decide to switch up our usual route and take Hank down to Sunset. When you're walking a dog, people just start talking to you. Usually I'm okay with it, but this morning I just want to be in my own head and think. What did Enrique mean by "more than the restaurant"? How did the psychic know so much about me?

I pass a diner where a bunch of scraggly-looking hipsters are eating eggs and bacon on street tables. Hank smells the bacon, and I have to use significant force to pry him away. Then he actually pulls me down an alley and pushes open a door with peeling green paint, almost like he's on a treasure hunt. I look around and see that we just came through the side entrance of a used bookstore. There's a box filled with old paperbacks and some hardcovers, and a homemade sign that says 25¢ with an arrow pointing to a piggy bank that has faded from pink to off-white. I leaf through the books while Hank finds what he was looking for: an old pizza box. Most of the books are cheesy romance novels and random things like manuals and gardening books, but there's one that draws me in. It's a medium-sized vintage cookbook. On the cover is a drawing of a woman's head with thought bubbles coming out of it. Judging by the font and style, I'd say it's from the sixties, and the title is *A Food for Every Mood*. As I flip through, I notice there are illustrations next to each recipe. On some pages, there are handwritten notes in the margins, presumably from the previous owner. I check my pocket and realize I only have sixteen cents. I plop the coins into the old piggy bank, hoping that will do. Hank looks at me like I'm a little strange, and to be honest, he may be right.

Before we leave, I hold the book in my hands, running my fingers across the cover. *You will have guidance from someone in the past.* I keep staring at the cover, wondering if the psychic knew I would find it or if I was somehow drawn to it because of what she said. Hank barks a little and I place the book safely in my bag.

When we get back home I put Hank in his crate in Davida's garage. He whines a little, and I actually consider bringing him to work, but I probably shouldn't try that on my first day.

Things at J. Tucker Casting start out smoothly, although I'm pretty nervous the whole time. Janice has me look through a huge file of head shots for a man in his thirties with long hair. I only find a few, but I put them on a thumb drive for her. I silently thank Bell for teaching me to be so

Apple proficient. Bell is addicted to Apple products. He was one of the crazy people lining up around the block for the first iPhone. Apple's the only thing he actually spends money on, besides food and wine. Then there's me—I'm, like, the only teenager in L.A. without a cell phone. Bell and Enrique have tried to get me to carry one, for emergencies, but I just refuse. Everyone is so attached to their phones, I find it liberating to not have one. I also kind of enjoy how people react when they find out, like I'm some kind of alien. I find it oddly reassuring that I'm a bit different. But mainly, I'm just not a phone person. I prefer to look up at the trees when I walk home, or stop by people's houses to actually talk to them face to face. Plus, some reports say cell phones cause brain cancer. I don't know if that's true, but I seriously doubt that being glued to your phone can be healthy.

Around noon I hear the silver door open, but no one's there. I peer over my desk and see a little person wearing a cowboy hat and a denim vest. Janice comes in and whispers in my ear, "I forgot to tell you. It's a commercial call for a little person dressed as a cowboy. There are four coming—just have them fill out the one-sheeter and wait." She slips back into her office without acknowledging the mini cowboy.

I do as I'm told, and, sure enough, three other mini cowboys come, and one is a woman with what looks like a bonnet on her head. What in the world could this commercial be for?

Thirty minutes later Janice comes out and hands me

the sides, again whispering in my ear. "I have a lunch at Paramount. Just have them each read the line and pick the top two. They'll be called back tomorrow for the director, same time."

It's strange that I'm being given this responsibility, but I start with the woman. The line is "Giddyup!" It's one of those moments when you ask yourself, *How can people just act like this is totally normal?* My red face must be quite a sight next to my already reddish hair.

Here's the thing I learn at my first casting session: auditioning is just as hard on the person casting as it is on the person auditioning. Each cowboy tries to outdo the previous one, and the "Giddyup!" line gets more and more frenetic and almost menacing. I have absolutely no idea who to pick, never mind the context of the commercial. I remind myself to tell Bell about this. He will find it hilarious.

I decide on the woman, because she seemed the most natural. Then I pick the man with blue eyes because he has a great smile.

After they leave it gets kind of quiet and I can't find any work to do, so I start to read my favorite food blogs. On the first one, Foodapalooza, a blogger from New York City talks about the rise of food trucks and how it was directly related to Twitter. A guy in Denmark who calls himself Soupdork writes about a trip he took across Europe, staying with people he met on Couchsurfer.com, and how he made soups from whatever was in each person's fridge.

One soup was made from mustard, two slices of ham, and a radish. I know it's silly, but I like reading stuff like this over Perez and Facebook. In addition to the no-cell-phone thing, I'm probably the only teenager in L.A. who doesn't have a Facebook page. I have a love-hate relationship with technology. Love blogs, hate social networking. I like the fact that I can email Soupdork for recipes, but I don't want to stare at pictures of my "friends" or read about boring movies or celebrity sightings. Most people in L.A. are obsessed with celebrities, but I honestly don't care. Just because someone is on a big screen and looks pretty in a dress doesn't mean she's an amazing person. There's a woman on my block who's a single mother to five boys, works three jobs, and creates these unbelievable paintings of foggy forests and rolling hills. With cheekbones that could cut glass and hips that make shade, she looks more beautiful than any movie star in the world.

The phone rings three times, and I take messages for Janice on the little pad that says WHILE YOU WERE OUT. Then Janice herself calls.

"Hey, kiddo, something's come up, and I won't be in for a while. Would you mind screen-testing a possible new client?" she asks.

"Sure, but—"

"The video camera is already set up in my office. Have him do two monologues—one drama and one comedy. If he doesn't have material, you'll find some in a pile on the back shelf."

"Okay."

"Just make sure he slates."

"What?"

"Have him state his name before he begins. Oh, and have him fill out the form—same one you did with the midgets—sorry, little people."

I go into Janice's office and check the video camera. Seems easy enough. Then I look for the monologues. Before I can even open the ones titled *Male—Teen to Early Twenties*, I hear a knock on the front door. It's an older woman with bleached hair in a black business suit. She has a rip in her stocking.

"Hi, I work upstairs, and a little bird mentioned Janice was looking for someone." She leans into me as if we're old friends. "I really want to get into the biz, you know? Behind the scenes."

"It's me" is all I say, which is a really weird response.

"What?"

They say sounds are one of the strongest sense memories, like how a song can take you immediately back to a scene in your past. In this case, I hear someone clear his throat, in a soft, polite way, and I'm instantly transported back in time.

He's standing behind the bleached-hair woman. It takes a second before I can see his face, but I already know it's him. Something in my chest tightens, as if I suddenly realize I'm on the edge of a cliff.

Theo.

Miraculously, the woman realizes Theo is upstaging her, and hurries off, muttering, "I'll stop by later."

I look at Theo and smile, but it feels forced. Smiling is the most natural thing you can do, but faking a smile may be the most awkward. He still looks like he's hiding something I want to know. His black hair is longer, spiky in a way that is either perfectly planned or completely random. Bedhead in real life, or Bedhead the product? Either way, when his green eyes go soft and he opens his arms, I am drawn into them by a magnetic force that takes me over. Now my smile is real. I look up at him and say, "What are you doing here?"

He backs away a little and hands me a head shot. "Long story. What are *you* doing here?"

"I work here. What happened to you last year? We were supposed to meet at the ninety-nine-cent store. Then you never came back to work." I suddenly have this horrible fear that he might not even remember, but he does.

"I can explain. Can you—can we—can I see you later?"

For what seems like the next few minutes, we just stare at each other. His acne has cleared, and he seems a little taller.

"I guess so," I say finally. "This is just . . ."

"Weird, I know," he says.

I lean against the bookcase and realize that his presence has somehow relaxed me. My body has gone languid.

"Do you remember my brother, Timothy?" Theo asks.

"No, not really."

"Well, he has mental disabilities, major. That day, when we were supposed to meet, they said he was being sent away, to Oregon. Some special institution. I had to take him . . . 'cause my mom . . . Like I said, this is a long story." His phone buzzes. "Can we do this later? I'll come back to read, too. I should really go. . . ."

I can see a cloud of emotion come over his face, so I just nod.

Then he says, "Maybe we could go somewhere, finish talking?"

"I'd like that." And I really would.

"What about the Griffith Park? Tomorrow? I haven't been since I was a kid."

"That sounds nice."

The phone rings, and I take another message for Janice. I hang up and look down at the photo he handed me. It looks a little retouched, but his gaze covers me slowly, like sheets falling from a clothesline.

"What?" he says.

I realize I am smiling.

"Nothing," I say.

But it's definitely not nothing.

CHAPTER 7

On my way out, instead of pressing 1 for the lobby, I press 12, the floor the psychic was on. Was Theo's walking into J. Tucker merely a coincidence? I search the doors on the floor. Insurance? Not likely. Lawyers? Nope. Just when I'm about to give up and turn around, I see one more office door at the end of the hallway. It says: TREE OF LIFE: MASSAGE, PILATES, ACUPUNCTURE. Now, *that* makes sense. As I raise my hand to knock, the psychic comes out, with that same confident look on her face, as if she had prepared for the scene. But she looks different. Her hair is pulled back tight, and her face is flushed.

"You returned," she says, with a smile so penetrating I have to glance away for a second. She walks toward the elevator, and I follow her inside. Now the two of us are back where we met, except this time the elevator's moving and I only have twelve floors to pick her brain.

"Listen, I know I was skeptical, but I think you're right. Something happened today—"

"I *am* a professional," she says, glaring at me with those clear eyes.

"Yes, obviously. But after I saw you, I got the job, and this boy Theo just showed up at my work, and yesterday I found this. It's from the past, like you said." I take out the cookbook, which I've had with me ever since I got it but for some reason have been wary of opening again, and show it to her. She grabs it and slowly closes her eyes. Then she says, "Where did you get this?" as if it could be a bomb that's about to go off.

"At a used bookstore. It was strange, this dog I walk, Hank—"

She holds up her hand as if the details are beneath her and have no relevance to what's really going on. She opens the front cover and we both see an indecipherable name, crossed out, and underneath, written in cursive: *Rose Lane, 18, 1966*. She closes the cover as well as her eyes and says, "This will be important to you, but something else will happen. Today. You will be given a sign, or shown a piece of something larger."

"Theo?"

"No, this hasn't happened yet." She opens her eyes, and her sincerity is gone. "You know, I really should be charging you," she says as she hands the cookbook back to me.

The elevator lets us out into the lobby, and I follow her, like she's got my future in her hands. She turns to me with a hint of pity but also maybe envy—I can't imagine why.

"I'm sorry, I can't give you all the answers." She starts to walk away, then turns back and says, "We won't meet again—not for some time. You will know what to do. Trust yourself."

The whole way home I look for signs. The old woman on the bus with mysterious eyes, the nervous man with the briefcase. Is she looking at me? What's inside the briefcase? Is the bus going to get hijacked? I look out the window and smile at my paranoia. I look again at the name inside the cookbook. I see that it was published in 1960. I wonder what it would have been like to be a teenager back then.

When I get home, the phone is ringing. It's Bell calling from the bank, and he needs me to read him some information from his closing documents on the house. He tells me to go into his room, to the little desk by the window. When we were kids, Jeremy and I were never allowed near this desk. It still feels a bit off-limits.

I find the documents, read Bell the information he needs, and hang up. As I put the folder back in the drawer, I notice the corner of a wooden box at the bottom. Bell's handwriting is on the top, spelling out my full name: *Olivia Anne Reese*. I pull out the box and place it on my lap, contemplating. What could this be?

I open it slowly, half expecting to see a small dead animal or something scary. But it's just some pictures of me as a baby, and a silver rattle. There are some adoption papers from the agency. None of them mention my mother's name. But the information must be somewhere in the world, right? Maybe in a dusty cabinet at the adoption agency in the Valley.

Just as I'm about to close the box, I notice a tiny manila envelope tied shut with red string. On the back it says NORTH HOLLYWOOD BANK AND TRUST. I open the envelope. Inside is a small key with 74C on it. It must be a safe-deposit box. At a bank right near my adoption agency. I take the key out and turn it around in my hand a few times. I can feel my heart speed up. Suddenly I hear the downstairs door open, and I scramble to put everything back, except for the key, which I put in my pocket.

I go downstairs and sit on the couch. I try to figure out what to make for Lola, who is coming over for dinner. But the key is like this small vortex of heat in my pocket. *A sign, a piece of something larger.*

As soon as he sees me, Bell can tell something's up. He's just here to change and leave for the restaurant, but he keeps stopping to stare at me, as if he's trying to figure something out. I decide to tell him about the job, now that I have it for sure. He gives me a proud smile and a hug. Then he picks up one of my feet and cradles it in his palm—a tender gesture he's always made—and says, "Working girl."

"Not that kind, Dad."

He smiles, puts my foot back down, and says, "Bravo."

After he leaves, I take the cookbook out of my bag. I open it to a random page. Next to a drawing of a woman singing on a mountaintop, there's a heading that reads CONFIDENT CARROT CAKE. The note scrawled in the margin was probably once in black ink but has faded to brown:

11/9/66

Made this for you, Matthew, as it would have been your second birthday. For those few minutes I held you, before the doctors took you away, I thought I could finally give Mother what she needed. Little did I know, it would only make things worse. I still carry you in my heart.

I look again at the inside cover. *Rose Lane, 18, 1966.* So she got pregnant at my age? I know people got married early back then, but was teen pregnancy normal? I try to picture a girl, maybe in a dress with a bold print, cooking carrot cake for the child she lost. Did her mother blame her? Hold it against her? How could you not love and support your own daughter? But I guess mine didn't even have a chance. Does she still think about me?

My thoughts are harshly interrupted by the door squeaking open, and for some reason I instinctively hide the book.

In comes Lola with the scent of chlorine in her hair. She's been swimming at her parents' club pool.

"You okay, Livie? You look like you've just seen a ghost."

"I'm fine. Just going to throw together a salad from what's in the fridge, okay?"

"Coming from you, Livie, it will most likely win some salad award regardless."

I go over to the fridge, grab a cucumber, and toss it to Lola. "Thin, like dimes."

"Right. You must tell me, though, how was your first day?"

I start washing the lettuce and tell her about the little people. Then, trying to play it down as an afterthought, I fill her in on the return of Dish Boy.

Lola stops chopping and says, "No!"

I start to fry up slices of prosciutto while mincing some garlic for the dressing.

"Yes. Crazy, right? We didn't have time to do the screen test 'cause he had to go help his brother, Timothy, who has some problems, but we made a plan to go to the Griffith Park tomorrow."

"How frightfully romantic!"

"I'm trying not to get too excited."

"Why did he disappear?"

"He's going to fill me in tomorrow. He acted like it all could be explained easily. Like, 'I just took off for a year, pass the butter.'"

I finish the salad—field greens, garbanzo beans, and feta

cheese, topped with cucumber, shallots, and crispy pro-sciutto. It's a weird combination, but it works. It's like this entrepreneur who spoke at our school said—you must always keep your mind open; half of the world's great ideas were born out of unlikely pairings. Dressings are the key to making salads sing, and usually all it takes is a really good olive oil, fresh black pepper, and high-end mustard. As we begin to eat, Lola is quiet, so I know it's doing the trick. A quiet dinner table equals a good cook.

When we're almost finished, Enrique comes home smelling of whiskey. I can tell he's buzzed 'cause his eyes, which are normally over-alert, aren't focusing very well. Enrique isn't the type to get drunk often, and the fact that he starts asking Lola about her earrings is be-yond awkward. I tell Lola we should go and she quickly obliges.

On our way down the hill to where Lola parked, she expresses what we're both thinking. "Well, that was a bit strange."

"Tell me about it."

"You know, it's funny, when I first came to the States I didn't know that expression, so when people said 'Tell me about it,' I used to take it literally, blabbing away. . . ."

In spite of everything, we start laughing. Some little kids who clearly shouldn't be out this late run by with sno-cones in their hands. Lola hugs me goodbye and gets into her black Mini Cooper. She tells me to call her the minute my date with Theo is over.

When I get back inside, I lie down on the couch and think through the whole Theo thing, and how maybe it's a sign, that he's back in my life. There is also the key, still burning a hole in my jeans. I can hear the psychic in my head. *Trust yourself.*

When Bell gets home, he doesn't see me and goes straight into the kitchen. He grabs a tumbler and fills it with scotch. The sight of him sitting alone in the dark dampens my mood. I get up from the couch and go sit next to him. He jumps in surprise, then offers me an apple. I decline.

He takes a long, slow sip and swallows.

"Dad, do you remember when you let me have a sip of that 'ninety-one Bordeaux?" I ask.

"Vaguely."

"It was your birthday. Jeremy had just graduated, and he had that really nice girl with him . . . Bridget? Anyway, I screwed up the skirt steak and was kind of mortified. You said it would be okay and let me take a sip of your drink. Papá showed up late but brought sparkling cider, and we all toasted, and I remember thinking, this isn't about overdone skirt steak or 'ninety-one Bordeaux. It's what we all are—together. We're kind of like a machine of mismatched parts." I'm not sure what to do for someone who has sacrificed so much for me, and I have no idea how to help him, but I'm improvising. "Remember, I have a job. And Jeremy's getting an ice cream truck."

Bell looks at me like I'm a five-year-old telling him that my stuffed-animal army will protect him.

"We'll figure it out," I say.

He offers me the apple again, and this time I take it.

When he hugs me, I hear something strange. A cough or some kind of whimper. I don't care to admit it, but it's most likely the latter. Bell is the architecture that holds our family up, and we can't afford for him to crumble.

When I was in fifth grade they had Bring Your Mom to School Day. Bell or Enrique could've come, but it didn't feel right and I didn't push the issue. In our classroom, we all had to play this game with our mothers, and the teacher pretended she was mine. It was the first time that I really *felt* not having a mother. I don't remember the details of the game, but I know that it didn't work. The mother had to know certain details about the child, and my teacher tried desperately to fill in, but it clearly wasn't happening. When I got home that day, Bell was trimming the bushes in front of our bungalow. He dropped his shears and ran up to hug me, but I dodged his arms.

"I had to have a mother, right, Dad?" I asked him.

He gave me that look of concern that sometimes makes me warm inside but right then made me queasy.

"Yes, of course, Ollie. You didn't fall from the sky."

I wasn't stupid. I had seen *Annie*. I knew that some kids

were given up for adoption and that was just the way it was. But I felt hatred for Bell, like somehow it was all his fault, which of course it wasn't.

"What did they say? They must have told you something about her."

Bell ran his hands through his hair, which was even thicker then and completely black. "I wish there was something I could tell you, Ollie, but I'm in the same boat as you. I know nothing."

"What about her name?"

He paused for a moment and looked up at the clouds. Then he kneeled down to my level and gave me that look of concern again.

"She requested to remain nameless."

"Figures," I said, walking past him and into the house.

I went up to my room and cried until it was time for dinner. When Jeremy came up to get me, he sat on the edge of my bed and scratched my back.

"So it was mom day or whatever?"

"Yeah."

"Look at it this way, sis. We kind of get to run our own show, you know? The Dads are on top of it, but we don't have a mother breathing down our necks."

He was right, but it still didn't make me feel better. I loved my family, but it wasn't fair.

"I just hate how they always say 'Get your mother's permission' or 'Call your mother.' It's like I'm constantly reminded, you know?"

"I know," Jeremy said. "But maybe one day you can have a kid and be your own mother."

His logic didn't really make sense, but it satisfied me for the moment.

After dinner that night, we all played charades. It was so funny watching Enrique try to give clues to American shows he barely knew. And Bell and Jeremy would get so competitive. Mostly, though, we laughed.

Now, lying on my bed at the end of a very long day, I listen to the empty house and realize that's what we've been missing. Laughter. For as long as I can remember, Enrique and Bell would always laugh together. They would play tricks on each other, and do impressions, and to me it seemed like they were such a perfect pair. But how well do we really know our parents? With everything going on with my family now, would finding my mother help or hinder the situation?

I think about Rose Lane, from the cookbook, how she and her mother must not have been close. I get it, the love between her and her mother was complicated, but there must have been something else. Did Rose betray her in some way? I can't imagine the loss Rose must have felt. Still, she found inspiration to cook, and to write. She held her son for a few minutes, just like my mother must have done. Was that a blessing or a curse? Are they one and the same?

I take out the old cookbook and hold it like the psychic did, as if she could never pretend to know its power. I flip to another random page. Next to a drawing of a woman jumping off a diving board, there's a recipe called JOYFUL JAMBALAYA, and another handwritten note in the margin:

1/14/67

Kurt seemed to like it, but there is something as thick as the jambalaya between us. It used to be so easy, now it's all so complicated. We never say his name. How could we?

Kurt must be Rose's husband. My mind starts to go full speed. What happened? Was she talking about Matthew? I don't know why, but I can tell this Rose was a good person. Or maybe she's still alive. Why was her mother never satisfied? I write my own note underneath hers:

You did the best you could, and that's all you can do.
You can thin out the jambalaya with beef stock.

Sometimes I like to hear people talking when I go to sleep. The words and meanings go away and it's just a voice, someone else out there in the world. I turn on the AM radio, and through the little speaker comes a voice, female, and I drown out the words, imagining it to be Rose's voice, telling me the story of how she met Kurt.

. . . We met at a county fair. Kurt covered me with his jacket after it started to rain. I refused, told him

I didn't mind getting wet, and off we went, running through the storm, spellbound. When the rain stopped, we sat in waterlogged clothes outside the gates. We laughed for no apparent reason. From that point on, we were inseparable. We went to a diner and ate breakfast at midnight. I was always myself around him.

CHAPTER 8

On Wednesday, my second day of work, Janice tells me I'm two days away from getting paid. She's paying me under the table. When I was younger and heard Bell was doing that with some of the dishwashers, I actually thought he meant it literally. I panicked when he plucked down some cash for one of them, right on top of the table.

All through work I think about Theo, and the key in my pocket, and whether the psychic knew what she was talking about or if she was just lucky. When it comes time to leave, I go into the bathroom and, once again, apply a touch of mascara and some lip gloss. He better not stand me up again, almost exactly a year later. That would be pathetic.

On my way to meet him at Griffith Park I stop off at Jeremy's place. He's not inside, but I hear his voice in the alley. He's down there with Phil, and they're looking under the hood of an ice cream truck. He's really doing it. The truck is pink and brown, with a rusted bumper. It says ICY COLD in big block letters, but nothing else. At one point it probably said ICY COLD TREATS or something. Suddenly, I change my mind about saying hi to Jeremy, and I sneak by without being seen. I'm too excited about my date with Theo to concentrate on anything else.

Back on the boulevard I notice the old art gallery. There's never anything in it, except for three retro TVs in the window, usually playing cartoons. Today, however, two of them are just playing black-and-white fuzz, and the other is playing an old movie. The movie I don't recognize, but the actress I do. It is unmistakably Julie Andrews. I look at her hair, her eyes—the only woman I've ever looked at and seen pieces of myself. I feel tears well up in my eyes, and I know: it's time. Even if she doesn't look like Julie Andrews, I've got to find out who my mother is. I take the key out of my pocket and hold it up to the glass.

Griffith Park is filled with people walking their dogs, joggers, and what Bell calls "randoms"—people who look a little lost, or high, or maybe mentally unstable. I find myself smiling at everyone, which is not a usual thing for me. I'm not much of a romantic, but I feel an inexplicable happiness, like maybe everything is going to be okay.

Theo is sitting on the stone wall by the conservatory. The buildings of downtown L.A. rise out of the sunset smog in the distance. Theo looks older somehow; I'm not sure why. But he is still "dead cute," as Lola would say. I sit down next to him and we watch the skyline, layers of orange trying to fight through the gray. When the sky becomes drained of color and only the smog remains, he turns to me and says, "I'm so sorry."

I just look into his green eyes, which are swimming with remorse. He starts talking softly.

"Everything came crashing down that day. My mother, she was going to send Timothy to this institution. She hardly spent any time with him. I basically raised him. I knew he would never last in a place like that. He was terrified of going. So instead, I faked out my mother and took him to my aunt's house in Seattle. It was one of those moments, I can't really explain it. I had to go. It was the only way. I knew you didn't have a cell phone. Do you have one now?"

"No. I suppose I will have to cave in at some point, but I'm trying to hold out."

He smiles a little funny, like he thinks it's cute I'm so removed from mass culture.

"Well, now Timothy and I are back home because my aunt sold her house and moved, and she's got some of her own problems to deal with. But I called you at your house, Liv. Did Enrique give you the message?"

"What? No."

"I really wanted to talk to you."

"I did too. I sat at the ninety-nine-cent store for like an hour."

He reaches out and pulls a stray hair off my face, and we stare at each other, wondering how the heck the universe brought us back together. We never really knew each other that well, but I'm glad he feels like he can confide in me. He wouldn't say all that personal family stuff to just anyone.

"You look great," he says.

I feel myself blushing, so I start to tell him about the restaurant.

"Oh no."

"It's pretty bad. Dad is in denial, I think. And Papá is just numbing himself with alcohol. It's really sad. I remember when Dad first opened the place, and Papá was designing the menus . . . there was so much happiness there. Now you walk in and you can feel this sense of doom. Like the ceiling's going to fall in or something."

"So what are you going to do?"

"Well, I'm working now, and Jeremy's got this ice cream truck. . . ."

Theo rolls his eyes, probably thinking about Jeremy's big talk about his band last summer. "Sounds promising."

Three large birds fly in perfect V formation right over our heads. I think of Julie Andrews on that small old TV, smiling so effortlessly.

"Grace," I say.

"What?"

"Those birds. It's amazing, isn't it? That they just spread their wings and boom, they're soaring above the earth. That's, like, the definition of grace."

"I guess that's why we fly in dreams," Theo says.

He looks at me differently, like maybe I have changed since last summer. Of course I have. We both have.

"I was so mad at you. I couldn't believe you'd just take off like that."

"It was complicated," he says. "Family, in most cases, comes first."

"So why did you call the house only once?"

"I thought—I thought you had your reasons for not calling me back. Like you didn't want to talk to me. And then I had my hands full up there. Timothy is not easy. You'll see."

You'll see. Does this mean we'll be hanging out more? I try to diminish the smile that is spreading over my face. After a bit, we start walking. He takes my hand, and at first it seems clumsy, but then I relax into it, and I feel like I'm floating. I think of my earliest memory, walking in Venice Beach with one hand in Bell's and the other in Enrique's. They would swing me up every few steps, and everyone who walked by smiled at us. There were people on Rollerblades, hippies selling incense, punk kids with pierced eyebrows and pink hair . . . it was basically a circus. And there at the center, in the calm of the storm, were my dads and me. It was one of those perfect moments.

"Do you believe in destiny?" I ask.

Theo turns his soft eyes on me and says, "How do you mean?"

I tell him about the psychic. I leave out the "young man" part.

"Sounds like something's definitely in the cards," he says. "No pun intended."

"I just have this feeling, like something is slipping away. I don't know, my innocence? It's like, when you're a kid the biggest worry is whether or not you can have ice cream after lunch, and then you become an adult, and real threats happen, like Dad losing the restaurant. And I've been thinking about the fact that there's a woman out there who gave birth to me who I don't know and maybe won't be able to find. It just feels like the foundation we've all built is breaking down."

"Tell me about it. My mother gave up on Timothy, and I'm the only reason he's still alive. When you're a kid everything is a fairy tale, or they lead you to believe that by the books they give you. . . . Then you realize life is, well, screwed up beyond belief."

We reach the end of the park and start walking down the sidewalk back toward Theo's neighborhood. We pass a couple on a bench, and the man kisses the woman's shoulder.

"The thing is, Liv, what is it *you* want?"

"What?"

"Well, from what I saw at the restaurant last year, you

always seem to be helping other people. But you need to figure out what *you* want. Like, what's your dream?"

"I've always wanted to go to Le Cordon Bleu in Paris, the famous cooking school. Not sure how the heck that would actually happen, though. It's got to be super expensive. My guidance counselor says I can totally get into college, but what's the point if I want to be a cook?"

Theo throws me that smile he used to give me, standing in his apron behind the dish rack at FOOD. "There's no reason you can't go to cooking school in France. Dreams happen."

We stop at a crosswalk and a tricked-out car filled with what looks like gang members pulls up, the bass thumping so hard I can feel it in my heart.

"Yeah, maybe to some people—people with money and—"

"To everyone," Theo says. "Maybe it starts out like a fairy tale, then everything gets jacked, then it all comes together in a happy ending."

"Listen to you, Mr. Positive."

"You have to be that way, sometimes, to survive."

We cross the street and start picking through a parking lot sale. I see a sad painting of an apple, some costume jewelry, and a trunk full of old matchboxes. Theo secretly buys a necklace, then slips it on me. It's blue, with small beads separated by spiky silver things. The color matches my eyes. It's not something I would normally wear, but because he puts it on me so sweetly, I fear I may never take it off.

When we get to the block of Sunset where we separate, I notice another flock of birds, this time maybe twenty of them in formation above our heads. *Grace.*

"What about you?" I ask him. "What's your dream?"

Theo studies his feet for a moment. Then he speaks, his voice shaky, as if he's been waiting a long time to have this conversation. "Well, I want to race on a team, get paid to cycle and see the world. And to have someone I can be myself around. Does that sound corny as hell?"

I look up and the palm trees are lean, proud soldiers, the one constant in my life.

"No. But tell me, did you see anyone else? Up in Oregon?"

He doesn't answer, just looks at me with what could be guilt or pity.

"The important thing is that we're here now, right?"

I look up at him, and he cups his hand under my chin, leaning in to kiss me. For that moment, I don't hear the cars or the birds or anything. My mind becomes as clear as an empty glass bowl.

CHAPTER 9

When I was five and Jeremy was seven, we had bunk beds that were shaped like racecars. I slept in the bottom car, and if I had a bad dream or something woke me up, I would push my feet against the bottom of Jeremy's mattress to make sure he was there. One time I pushed and there was no resistance, so I panicked. I grabbed my blankie and walked into the living room to find Jeremy staring at the front door. I asked him what he was doing and he said, "Waiting for Papá." At the time, I had no idea why he'd be doing such a thing, but now I realize that was the first time Enrique and Bell had a spat and Enrique left. Jeremy was devastated. I was too young to really know what was going on, but I do remember Jeremy on the brink of tears, and just wanting the good to be restored in the world.

It's around ten p.m. I've just gotten off the phone with Lola, giving her the details of my date with Theo. I lean back on the couch and close my eyes. I can hear Davida singing to Hank, and the scrape and roll of kids skateboarding under the streetlights. Just when I doze off, the slap of the screen door jolts me awake. Enrique is in his usual preppy outfit and has not been drinking. I know this because he looks me right in the eye.

I glare back at him and he looks surprised. "What is it? You are mad with me?"

"You remember Theo, the dishwasher?"

"Yes, I think."

"Do you remember when he just disappeared?"

"A little."

"Well, he said he called and left a message for me. That you were the one who took the message."

Enrique smiles, as if this problem is nothing to be alarmed about. A scraped knee fixed with a Band-Aid. "Oh, Ollie, I am so sorry. I don't remember. Maybe I was—"

"Wrapped up in your own world?"

He smiles again, but this time like a scolded puppy. "Not fair, Ollie. I—I know I can be . . . like that. . . ."

What is it with people and their smiles? How can they hold so much weight?

"Well, I just want you to know something: the things you do, or forget to do in this case, affect the people around you—a lot. And even though I'm upset about this, it's nothing compared to what's going on with Dad. He needs you. Please, just be nice to each other. I can't stand the tension around here."

There's water collecting in Enrique's eyes. He gets a beer and brings me some orange juice in a coffee mug. He knows it's basically the only thing I drink. When I was a toddler he once bought orange Gatorade by mistake and I wasn't having it. I spit it out right in the middle of a crowded bus. He tells the story all the time.

"We have to help Dad," I say.

"Bell, Bell, Bell."

"What?"

As if we are on the set of a sitcom, Bell walks in. He looks tired but, as Lola says, charming—a poor man's George Clooney. He doesn't say anything but looks at us both in his way, distant yet concerned, a walking duality. He goes into the kitchen and comes back with a glass of milk. We each sit silently, together and alone, sipping our drinks and wondering what will become of us.

I end up falling asleep on the couch but once again am disturbed by the screen door. It's Jeremy. It must be after midnight, but he's got fire in his eyes and sweat stains on his T-shirt. He starts pacing.

"Ol, I'm glad you're here. I signed the demo deal. A thousand dollars! I bought the truck, and now I can get supplies. Should be up and running by the end of the week. And check this out—we hacked into the system and changed the annoying ice cream music. Now it's this trippy jingle. Anyway, I'm stoked, it's gonna rake in cash, I can feel it."

This is always how it goes with Jeremy, and I'll encourage him as always because he's my brother, even while knowing that there are holes in his plans. He seems so pumped I don't ask him if he's even old enough to run his own business.

He sits down next to me and gives me a little hip check.

"You look different. Are you in love?"

"Shut up. But listen, I'm curious about something. I know you used to ask the Dads about your birth parents. . . ."

"Yeah, and they kept telling me they wanted to remain nameless."

"Me too!"

Jeremy looks hesitant, then starts talking. "Look, I didn't want to tell you then, but the day I turned eighteen, I tracked down the info through my friend whose dad works at the public records office. And it turns out they're dead. My mom died when I was a kid, and my real dad died a few years ago. Good times, eh?"

"I know my mother isn't dead. I don't know how, but I do. I can feel it."

"But what does it matter, Ol?"

"I'm not sure why it matters, but it does."

Jeremy throws up his hands, then asks, "What's the deal with the Dads?"

"Papá isn't on the couch."

"What?"

"Nothing, just tell me about the demo deal."

Jeremy gets up again, fiddling with his hair and scratching his cheek. He looks a little freakish. I think again about Bell saying we don't choose our family. What made my mother choose *not* to have one?

"I convinced them to let two of the songs be mine. And the other two will be that cougar chick's tunes."

"Great. You doing 'Hole in the Sky'?"

"You know it."

I get up and stretch a little, then give him a hug.

"I really need to sleep. Like, in a bed."

"Okay, Ol, let's try and meet up tomorrow," he says.

"Sounds good."

Jeremy heads to the door but then stops before he opens it. He turns around and says, "You met someone, didn't you?"

"It's a long story," I say, touching my blue necklace.

"I bet. Night, sis."

"Night."

Even though I'm exhausted, when his footsteps are gone, I find the cookbook and check randomly again, leaving it all to fate. In the margin next to a recipe for COOL CASSEROLE, I see Rose's now-familiar hand:

This came out bland. I forgot to season the macaroni. Even though I know he didn't like it, Kurt told me it was great. Over two years have passed and we still haven't said his name. He did ask me about Mother, though, and I told him the truth. He slowly shook his head.

This note makes my eyes water and my stomach queasy. Kurt complimenting Rose's casserole is like the birds: grace. Maybe it would have been better if they had said his name, put it out on the table for everyone to see. Simple, like bread and butter. I know it's not simple, but maybe if they treated it that way it would have been.

Again, I write my own note underneath Rose's:

If only we could cook our way out of everything.

I walk up to my room quickly and slip into bed, turning on my AM radio. I can't stop thinking about Rose, and Kurt, and her mother, and about where the key might lead me. Finding my mother seems like this impossible thing in the distance, like seeing a castle from a plane. But maybe it's getting closer. It might even be as simple as going to the bank. But for some reason, I don't want to go until I see Theo again, and it's only when I think of him that I can finally get to sleep.

CHAPTER 10

When I come downstairs in the morning, Bell has just gotten back from running. He's sitting at the small kitchen table, panting a little too hard. I get some juice and start cutting up a mango I got at the street market. He watches my technique like he's fascinated, but I think he just needs a distraction. I decide to further distract him by telling him about work and reconnecting with Theo.

"He's a good egg," Bell says. "I'm glad."

"It's weird, though—he's on this acting path now. I never pictured myself dating an actor."

"I thought he was into cycling?"

"That mostly, but he also wants to be repped by Janice."

"Which would technically mean you'd be romantically involved with one of your clients."

As if on cue, Enrique walks in and says, "We all know how that one goes."

The story is slightly different depending on who tells it, but when Bell first met Enrique, Bell was running a catering company and Enrique's dance company had hired it for their tenth anniversary. Apparently, Bell got the menu wrong because of a miscommunication. Bell says it was because of Enrique's accent, which was much thicker at the time, but Enrique says it was because Bell had two martinis during their initial meeting. They ended up having a very heated argument in front of all the guests, before taking it into the stairway of the reception hall to be private, and that's where it gets murky. From what I know, Enrique started to cry, and Bell held him in the stairway while the party raged on inside. Eventually they came back and danced together, to everyone's raised eyebrows.

Now Bell raises *his* eyebrows and heads upstairs to shower. Enrique grabs a couple pieces of my mango and sighs, sitting down where Bell just was. I tell him about Jeremy's ice cream truck, and how we both plan to save the restaurant.

"That is sweet, Ollie, but it's a lost cause."

I stop chewing the mango and give him a serious look. "What do you mean, Papá?"

Before he can answer, the phone rings. I can tell by his serious tone it's going to be a long call, but I wait, anxious. It's so like Enrique to drop a bomb and not think about the destruction. When he finally hangs up, I say, "Lost cause?"

He looks at me with what some might say is condescension, but then I can tell he wants to take it back.

"Sorry, Ollie, I'm not myself today. It will be fine. I'm glad you guys want to help out."

I don't really have the energy to inquire further, so I try my best to believe him.

"Can I give you a hypothetical?"

He nods. This is how he used to start a lot of conversations with me, and now it's my turn.

"Say my birth mother didn't remain nameless. Would you not want me to contact her?"

He looks at me deeply, as if I'm changing before his eyes, which I suppose I am. "Ollie, we can't really stop you from doing anything. We can only advise you and protect you as best we can."

"It's cool, I was just wondering."

The next week seems to fly by. I don't hear from Theo, but I know he had to go back to Oregon to get the rest of his stuff. Once in a while I get panicky and impatient that I haven't heard from him, but I know he has a lot to deal with up there, and before he left, he promised to call the day he gets back. So most of the time, I just float around in a happy haze and think about seeing him again.

At J. Tucker Casting, the mood is brighter. Janice is all

smiles, and she's humming a lot. Apparently she was hired to cast a big movie at Paramount, and it looks like she's going to sign Tom Hanks as the lead.

This morning is a casting day, so after rounding up a file of head shots for a 7UP commercial, I send the files to Janice electronically even though she's on the other side of the door. I'm getting pretty adept at navigating the casting software and the J. Tucker email server. I look out the window at another clear blue sky, with only one wisp of a cloud barely noticeable.

Janice opens the door and brings me some fancy chocolate.

"A client gave me these. Unlike me, you are young enough that they won't immediately become love handles."

"Oh, c'mon. You have, like, no body fat."

She smiles, checking herself out in the mirror behind me, then says, "I'm keeping you in the act."

Janice is one of those people who will remain happy if you constantly praise her.

"Have you ever been to Paris?"

She laughs. "Are you kidding? Of course. The only problem is there are too many French people."

"I want to go to Le Cordon Bleu, you know, the cooking school?"

"Ah, yes. Well, from the taste of that eggplant lasagna you brought in the other day, I would safely say you hardly need much training."

"Couldn't hurt, though, right?"

She examines a piece of the chocolate, sniffs it a little, and then puts it back in the box.

"No, it couldn't. But are you telling me you're ready to throw away your budding casting career for the culinary arts?"

I take a small bite, letting the chocolate melt a little on my tongue.

"Yes."

She pretends I've stabbed her in the heart and then retreats to her office. I retrieve my cookbook and set it on my lap. I think about Hank leading me into that alley and through that green door with the peeling paint. I can almost smell the scent of the psychic woman. *Be aware of your choices.*

I open to a recipe for RIGHTEOUS RATATOUILLE. Rose's note in the margin reads:

3/7/66

Made this for Kurt.
After, we danced.
For the first time, I spilled wine on my blouse and didn't care.
What is getting into me?

A flourish swells inside my chest. Why do I feel like I know this woman? I touch the handwritten part with my finger, and I can feel my face turn red. It wasn't really about the ratatouille. The food was just the beginning.

I call the secretary at Paramount for Janice, and it isn't until after I hang up that I realize my fingers are still clutching the book, marking the page. After they had the ratatouille, she must have made love to Kurt. This is dated earlier. Is that when she conceived the little boy, Matthew?

On my way home I pick up the ingredients for the ratatouille. While I'm in the kitchen preparing, no one is around, and I'm able to go to that other place—as Bell would say, I'm in the zone.

In the end, I add a little honey to counteract the garlic. Bell and Enrique come home and must smell the dish because they sit down as though this dinner were planned. They don't say much, but I can tell they like it. If there's one thing I've learned from Bell, it's how to forgive. I don't really know what's wrong between them, and he's not ready to run through the fields with Enrique, who disappeared again for a few days this week, but I can tell by their body language that Bell's starting to let him back in. I picture Rose spilling the wine, something inside her giving way, loosening.

After we're done, Bell grabs me for a dance while Enrique hums an old Spanish tune. Once again, food has brought us together. I try to send a secret message out into the universe to Rose: *You are good enough.*

When everything is washed and put away and there's no one but me in the kitchen, I open the cookbook to the inside cover and stare again at the curvy letters: *Rose Lane.* What a beautiful name.

CHAPTER 11

Now that I'm a working girl, the laundry has piled up, but I have some time before I have to go to FOOD to make my Saturday special. I can barely lift the bag on my way down our street. Two cars slow and offer me a ride. The drivers are both older guys, so I immediately decline, wishing I'd asked Lola to pick me up at my house when we spoke last night, rather than meet me at the Laundromat.

Lola is already there when I arrive and helps me sort the colors from the whites. She notices that I'm still wearing my necklace.

"Are you going to see him again?" she asks coyly.

"Yes." I smile sheepishly. "He called me this morning to say he's back from Oregon. We're going out tomorrow."

"Well, well, wasting no time, I see. You're glowing, by the way."

First Jeremy, now her. Why is everyone saying that?

"Well, I know it's been a year and I hardly know him, but I do feel a connection with Theo."

"That's so great, Livie."

Lola points to a pair of Enrique's tightie-whities and says, "Aren't these a bit boyish?"

"That's Enrique for you."

I show her a pair of Bell's boxers, and she says, "Now, those are classy."

I realize she's just described my dads by their underwear. As we get the loads into the washers, I imagine Rose doing laundry for Kurt. I like having Rose all to myself, but I can't hold her world in any longer. I decide to tell Lola everything. I tell her about Rose's book, and the note about Matthew. Then I tell her about seeing Julie Andrews on the TV in the gallery, and the key, how it all seems like some sort of sign, or a bunch of little signs leading to something bigger.

"Wow! This psychic woman must have been the real thing."

"It's weird, Hank *led* me to the bookstore. I've never even taken him on that route before. I also was forced to cross the street on the gallery side because the sidewalk was closed. And I found the key, like, twenty minutes after she told me there would be a sign."

"What do you think it all means?"

"Not sure, but I do know one thing. I want to find my mother. And I want you to help me."

"Of course, Livie. But come, let's go next door, this place stinks."

I look around. There's just a goth-looking girl and an old lady folding her sheets. "Okay."

As we walk outside I hear this strange sound, like a dying music box. I look across the street and see the ice cream truck.

"Oh my God, it's Jeremy!"

"No. Don't tell me. . . ."

Lola is skeptical but follows me as I jaywalk the boulevard. There are four kids crouched around and Jeremy is handing them treats. He has a funny hat on and is oversmiling like a maniac.

After the kids leave, he sees me and yells, "Ol! Check it!"

I look inside the truck. It's pretty barren save for an old silver cooler. He hands me and Lola each an ice cream sandwich, and Lola hands him a five-dollar bill, saying, "Keep the change, babe."

"I only have ice cream sandwiches and MoonPies, but ladies, they are moving fast. I've sold a hundred in three hours!"

Lola and I look at each other.

"I know what you're thinking. I applied for a license. It takes six weeks. So right now I'm on the down-low."

"On Sunset and Western?" I ask.

"You're right. I am headed over to Los Feliz. Apparently it's untapped territory."

I allow myself a smile. As crazy as he is, Jeremy does make stuff happen. The remixed jingle stops and starts again. He looks around for any more potential customers, then starts to shut the side counter.

"Well, ladies, it's been real. I've got to go spread some more ice cream love."

After he pulls away, Lola and I sit on a bench and eat our ice cream sandwiches.

"I hope there's not, like, razor blades in these or something," Lola says.

"No, just cyanide," I reply.

We cross the street and switch the laundry to the dryers. The goth girl is painting her fingernails black and the old lady is talking to herself. While the clothes dry we walk to the farmers' market and I try to figure out what to buy for my Saturday-night special. The yellow tomatoes look so amazing I decide on bruschetta. I pick up some elephant garlic, several loaves of french bread, and a bunch of fresh basil.

We head back to the Laundromat, and Lola helps me fold the laundry and bring it back to my house. When we get there I see a postcard stuck in the screen door. It's a black-and-white picture of a street in Paris. I turn it over.

Liv the Dream
—Theo

Lola looks over my shoulder and gasps. "So romantic!"

"I guess so," I say, but I'm biting my lip to hold back an enormous grin.

After I put the laundry away and Lola leaves, I find myself sitting quietly in the living room, staring at the postcard, almost believing in things previously unimaginable. I'm going to see Theo again tomorrow. And then maybe I'll see what I can find out at the bank.

FOOD is pretty empty when I get there, just a few prep chefs and Bell, who's on his knees scrubbing the baseboards. Not a good sign. He stands up and wipes his brow. "What are you making tonight?"

I hold up the yellow tomatoes. "Bruschetta."

He smiles, a real Bell smile, and for a moment I look around the restaurant, the space that contains so many memories for all of us, and try not to think about how it all could be taken away.

"Ollie, I have some news!" Bell says excitedly. "Enrique is coming in with some movie executives. He may have caught a break! A consulting gig for a film. Can you believe it?"

"Really? That's huge. How did that happen?"

"Well, when he took off"—there's only a slight edge to Bell's voice when he says this—"apparently he went sailing with a client, and they had lunch with a studio head, and he worked his magic."

"That's so great, Dad!"

I give Bell a hopeful smile, then let him get back to scrubbing—not a bad sign, after all—and go to set up my ingredients and cooking utensils. I begin by chopping the tomatoes super small and marinating them in fresh lemon juice. The key to bruschetta is to rub the bread with garlic. It's a subtle touch that makes all the difference. I let myself relax as my fingers peel the silky cloves. I wonder if Enrique is trying to do his part too. Without every flavor of our family working together, there is no dish.

There's a window from the kitchen that looks into the main dining room. I can see some of the waiters setting up, and toward the front door Bell is talking to two guys in suits. I assume they're from the bank. They hand Bell a piece of paper, and he smiles at them and shakes their hands. Even in the direst of circumstances, Bell is a gracious person. Like Rose. I bet after she lost the baby, she made Kurt dinners that were laced with kindness and sprinkled with hope.

The dinner rush happens late, but we are all thankful for the business. Enrique comes in with people from New Line Cinema, and toward the end of their meal, he waves me over. The men are middle-aged and have that moneyed, powerful look. Enrique introduces them to me, and I realize the second one, Len, is the head of the studio—I've called his office for Janice and spoken to his secretary many times. He's wearing diamond cuff links and glasses that are so thin they're almost invisible. He gives me a smile that seems sincere, and I try to return it.

"Len here is in love with your bruschetta," Enrique says, beaming proudly. I hope this is all for real for Enrique, and not a onetime thing like last time.

"It's nothing," I say, trying to play it down.

"Not only beautiful and a good cook," Len says, "but humble, too. You're batting a thousand."

"Len is from Tuscany, and he claims it's better than his mother's," Enrique says.

"Well, I'm sure your mother can make a killer meatball," I say, not sure what I'm even talking about.

"In fact, that's her specialty. Perhaps you two can exchange recipes sometime."

"Yeah, I get to Tuscany a lot."

The whole table laughs.

"Well, it was great to meet you," I say. "Try the chocolate torte if you're not too full."

As I walk away, I realize Bell is within earshot and heard my little spiel.

"Since when are you a comedian?" he whispers to me as we head toward the kitchen.

"Well, he's the head of New Line. And we need all the help we can get."

He stops and turns to me, looking right into my eyes.

"Ollie, you are turning into quite a woman, you know that?"

I can feel myself blush a little. "Well, I learned from the best."

He opens the door to the kitchen, and as we go in, the sous chef yells, "Fire four more bruschetta!"

Bell turns and heads back toward his office, but not before I hear him whisper, "That's my girl."

CHAPTER 12

Theo takes me to this place where you can paint your own dishware. It's really cute. He must have put some real thought into where our date should be. He chooses a giant bowl, and I opt for a mug. We sit down at a large circular table where there are two young girls across from us. The first thing I do, of course, is spill the red paint. The girls giggle, and a large woman in a shapeless dress comes over to help me clean it up and says, "Don't worry, it happens all the time."

"Can't take her anywhere," Theo says, winking at me. Then he gets this adorable, embarrassed look on his face. He spills a little of his blue paint on purpose, and the last bit of hurt and anger that I've been holding on to this past year evaporates.

"I'm not a good painter," I say.

"Don't worry. I drew a lobster once in fifth grade and everyone thought it was a dog."

"What?"

"Don't ask. But I'm making this for you, so you're just gonna have to live with it."

Theo reaches for the yellow paint, and his hand brushes my arm. The touch feels electric.

"So, is this a weird date or what?" he asks.

"No, it's great."

"I mean, I could have taken you to, like, a movie or something, but I guess I'm sick of doing the same old things over and over, you know?"

"I do. It's like these girls in my school. They go to the same mall every Friday and buy the same trendy bags and put on too much makeup. You'd think they'd get tired of it—doing the same things, being the same people."

"Yeah, there are kids at my school, guys who do that too. Like having the same pair of Nikes that everyone else has makes you the coolest kid in school. Please. Those people, you know, I hang out with them, but I always feel like there's something missing."

"Yes!" I say a little too enthusiastically.

"That's one of the things I like about you. Your clothes, your style . . . you're different in a good way, if that makes sense."

I shrug. "It just seems like such a waste of time to always try to be someone I'm not. Like trying to be some perfect version of the American teenager."

"No one's perfect. And neither is this bowl, I'm afraid." Theo shows me some paint dripping where he put on too much.

I think about imperfections, and how we're all basically made up of them. But sometimes on the right day, or in the right light, things can feel perfect. Like now.

My mug for Bell looks a little strange, but I'm sure he'll like it. He always says homemade presents are the best.

Even with the drips, Theo's bowl for me turns out really pretty, with washes of blue and yellow.

"It's beautiful," I tell him. "You work better as an abstract artist."

He laughs. "Yeah. Well, the next time you're whipping something up in the kitchen, you can think of me." He gives me a kiss, quick but soft.

"I don't think that will be a problem, bowl or no bowl," I say, grinning.

We take our masterpieces to the diner across the street, and the waitress almost pours coffee in my mug. Theo orders a grilled cheese and I get the chicken caesar. I realize halfway through that I probably shouldn't be eating garlic. Thankfully, I remember I have Altoids in my bag.

"This cheese is good, but strange. Want to try it and tell me what it is? I have no idea," Theo says, holding out half of his sandwich. I take a bite, and before I even swallow I know the answer.

"Gouda," I say.

He waves the waitress down and confirms it.

"That's awesome," he says. "You're like a food psychic."

"No, I just know my cheese."

"You know your food. And I can't wait to taste more of it. I'm supposed to eat a ton of carbs the nights before I train. Will you cook for me sometime?"

I blush a little. Pasta is kind of boring to make, but I'll do it every night if it's for Theo.

"Sure," I say, trying not to seem too excited.

Theo pays the check while I'm in the bathroom and opens the door for me when we leave. Then, even though it's way out of the way for him, he walks me all the way home.

When we get to my door, he kisses me again and says, "Liv, this has been so cool."

"Yes, it has. And thanks again for the bowl."

"It was made with . . . care."

I thought he was going to say *love*, almost saw his mouth forming the word, but then he just smiles, and so do I, and he turns to walk back down the hill. I watch him for a minute, taking deep breaths to try to calm my rapidly beating heart.

When I walk into the kitchen, I see Davida, tears rolling down her cheeks.

"Hank," she says, and I can tell it's something really bad.

"What?"

She takes in a few quick breaths in succession, as if she's catching them.

"In his sleep, last night. I guess it's sort of like a brain aneurysm."

A hundred thoughts crowd my brain. *Who will she sing to? Did he know he was going to die? One of the last things he did in life was lead me into that bookstore.* . . .

"Oh, Chef, he was my one and only."

I have been walking Hank for almost five years, since he was just a puppy. It's so hard to imagine him gone.

I sit down next to her, and the two of us cry silently.

After a minute, I get up and pour us each a glass of water. Davida clears her throat and says, "It's strange. When I found him, he was smiling."

"So at least it was peaceful, right?"

Davida gulps the water and stands up. "I'm going back to North Carolina for a while. It's time I visited my folks anyway, before they die on me too."

We both laugh a little, because sometimes it's the only way to see through the cloud of such a tragedy. Hank was the sweetest dog I've ever known. I don't tell her that, but I do give her a long hug and three slices of the banana bread I made yesterday.

The next morning, Lola drives me to work. Immediately, she knows something is wrong with me, so I tell her about

Hank dying, and something releases inside my chest, and I start to sob. It makes me feel like a total idiot. When I finally calm down, Lola says, "When I was seven, my hamster died and I didn't go to school for a week."

I don't tell her that it's hard to compare a hamster to a dog, partly because of the look on her face—like she's still mourning the loss—and partly because someone like Rose, who lost a child, might say the same thing to me about a dog. Maybe a pet and a person are one and the same, and it's really about how much love you have for the creature that suddenly leaves you for good.

Before I go to the casting office, I linger a little on the twelfth floor and think about finding the psychic again, but I don't. After what she said during our last encounter, I don't think I'd be able to find her anyway. When I get to my desk, I sit down and throw my bag on the floor. I notice the spine of the cookbook spilling out. I turn to the inside cover and look at Rose's signature again. I picture her in a swirly, bright dress, over which she wears an apron passed down from her grandmother. Her face has that open, healthy look that somewhat homely young wives had in the sixties. Maybe it was easy for her, though, having everything laid out at such a young age. Until, of course, Matthew slipped through her fingers. But I also see her as a walking contradiction. Maybe from the outside you couldn't see all the way in to where the edge lived: a daring, wild soul that sometimes showed its color. I flip to another page and there's a cute drawing of a boy sitting against a small tree. The heading reads CALMING CUCUMBER SOUP.

In the margin, there's a note:

4/19/68

> *Made this for Kurt. He leaves tomorrow.*
> *There is no food in the world that could calm the*
> *storm inside me. When I married him, I could never*
> *have imagined him leaving me, especially not for a war.*

Wow. Kurt went to war? I tell myself to breathe, that these people and their troubles have nothing to do with me, they are merely remnants in a book. Yet I can't believe this. What else can happen to this girl?

When I dropped Hank off after that walk, I never would have imagined that the end was so close. Hank was a wonderful dog. He had deep brown fur and an energetic gait. Everyone loved him, including me. I have never really had to deal with loss, besides not having a mother, but she was never there to begin with, and you can't lose something that was never there. But it's almost worse, never knowing.

Why did Kurt have to go? For how long? Couldn't he have just moved to Canada or something to avoid the draft?

Below Rose's note, I write:

Hope he came back.

I do my duties on autopilot, and Janice is really busy and hardly notices me. When Lola picks me up, I fill her in on my date with Theo and my whole Rose fantasy, and how I think it's somehow connected to me finding my mother, and my hunch that there's a bigger reason Theo suddenly reappeared. I tingle just mentioning his name, and I'm surprised I have room to think about anything else after our date. Even though she loves to talk, Lola has an inherent talent for listening.

"Well, Livie, I think the first order of business is ice cream. The real stuff, none of Jeremy's plastic-wrapped sandwiches. Then we'll make a plan."

A classic strategy: distraction. It actually works. Lola gets Oreo cookie and I get double chocolate crunch. We sit on a bench watching the hipsters go by.

"I know it's a bit maddening," she says, "but you can't try and figure everything out at once. Your dads have everything under control. I mean, they're not rich, but they make things work. Livie, they raised you to be the amazing person you are! Not too shabby."

I smile and lose a bite to the sidewalk.

"At least everything sounds great with Theo."

"You know what's weird? If we were dating in the sixties, we might be thinking about getting married right now."

"I'd start with a boyfriend before thinking about a husband. Anyway, your mother, now, that's something we should act on. If you really want to find out, or find her, then we should. Right?"

"Will you be my partner in crime?" I ask, knowing she'll agree.

"Well, how about a copilot? That sounds less incriminating. What bank is the key from?"

"North Hollywood Bank and Trust."

"Okay, let me do some research. Let's meet tomorrow—outside your office right after you get out of work. Bring the key."

"Sounds great. Thanks, Lola, for everything."

She drops me at my bank, and I deposit most of the first of the money I've made this summer, saving it for Bell. I keep the rest and pick up the ingredients for the cucumber soup.

When I get home and start unpacking the groceries, I already feel myself getting in the zone. I sauté the garlic and onion, add some lemon juice, and pour in the vegetable broth. I chop the cucumbers, fast at first, then slower. If I ever needed calming, it's right now. And, sure enough, as I cook, I feel that sense of peace that nothing else brings me, cloaking me in safety.

The soup calls for only salt and pepper, but I decide to add some cayenne as well. I transfer it all to the blender and add avocado and parsley, then slowly stir in the yogurt. It comes out beautifully. Perfect texture and just the right amount of kick.

I sit in the living room, a bowl of it on my lap. I am certainly calm, but I know it's just a matter of time before things get chaotic again. The trick is to enjoy the quiet moments in between. While I'm eating the last spoonful of the soup, the phone rings and startles me enough that I spill a few drops on the couch.

Flustered, I scramble to pick up. It's Enrique, I can tell by his breathing.

"Ollie, it's me. I'm at the police station."

CHAPTER 13

"What! Why? What happened?" I can't breathe.

"It's Jeremy. He's been arrested."

"I'm coming."

I slam the phone down and run to the station, which is only a few blocks away. Enrique is there, but Jeremy can't be released until Bell shows up. When I ask Enrique where Bell is, he just shrugs.

It turns out that the ice cream truck Jeremy bought was stolen, and his driver's license was expired, and he didn't have a permit to sell the ice cream, and there was beer involved. . . . Basically my brother is in deep crap. I feel bad for not seeing this coming or doing something to stop it. I tell Enrique as much, and he says, "Ollie, Jeremy is his own person. You cannot be responsible for everyone."

I let his words hang in the air, giving them a chance to sink in. "I just can't believe him. He never learns. How much is the bail?"

"I don't know, but we don't have it."

I walk up to the clerk lady, state my name and Jeremy's, and ask how much his bail is.

"Five thousand dollars."

"What?"

She looks past me to the next guy in line. I sit down next to Enrique, and Bell finally shows up a few minutes later. He looks frantic.

"Is he okay?"

"Yes, but Dad, if we haven't got five grand they're not going to let him go," I say.

We all sit there for what seems like a long while but could be ten minutes. Then we go home. The whole time, I avoid eye contact with Bell. He looks too defeated. But when I go to say good night, I hug him extra tight.

For some crazy reason, I sleep really well and wake up after my dads have left. I barely have time for juice as I rush out the door. But something stops me: a postcard, falling at my feet from inside the screen door. Again it's a black-and-white photograph of a street in Paris. There's a small dog, and someone walking a vintage bike. I smile and turn it over to read:

Liv the Dream—
See you at BEAN
Tomorrow night at 7:45
i'll be the one smiling.
                    —Theo

In the afternoon, Janice hands me an advance on my next paycheck. It's a little over three hundred dollars. It's sweet of her, but it's not going to get my stupid brother out of jail.

I quietly call Enrique on his cell.

"What's going on?" I ask.

"The public defender said if we can prove to the police that Jeremy bought the car and didn't steal it, they'll drop that charge and the amount of the money for bail. So Bell has been there since five a.m. trying to get him out."

"Okay, keep me posted."

Janice comes out and starts briefing me on the film she's casting, the big one, the one I've been waiting for her to clue me in on, but I'm too distracted to care. Why is my family such a bunch of screwups? I usually have this way of letting things roll over me, but right now I'm just plain sick of it. And I'm so angry at Jeremy for stressing out our dads even more than they already were.

I hear the names Reese Witherspoon and Shia LaBeouf, something about an exotic location, and a "budget with open faucets." Janice keeps on talking, and once again I notice how attractive she is, even with the taut ponytail and boyish sports coat. She finishes and looks at me expectantly, then says, "So?"

I have no idea what she's referring to. "I'm sorry, I missed the question."

"Can you call all these people on this list and give them their time slots?"

"Yes, sorry."

The rest of the day can't go by fast enough. I do more busywork, which I'm thankful for, and at five on the dot, I meet Lola at the corner. As she drives us east on Sunset, I show her the key.

"Great! And while you've been at work, I've gone all Veronica Mars."

"What do you mean?"

"Well, my father's mate is a high-level executive at North Hollywood Bank and Trust. I thought so when you told me the name, but I had to check to be sure. I explained everything to him, and he called in a favor and said you could have a couple minutes, but you'll be screened on your way out. I suppose that means they just want to make sure you haven't stolen anything."

"Seriously?"

"Yes. He said the people at the bank could lose their jobs for listening to him and letting you have access 'cause it's totally illegal, but I explained that it's just a name you're after."

I stare at Lola in her white scarf and big black glasses, looking like Jackie O's long-lost British granddaughter.

"I know. I want to know. Even if she's, like, a homeless person or a crackhead."

"Well, if she has half a brain, which, knowing you, I'm sure she does, she'll probably have a respectable lot in life."

I grab the key out of my pocket and stare at it to make sure it's real.

As we drive the 101 into North Hollywood, I try to calm myself down. It's just a name, like she said. It doesn't mean everything has to change. But I can't help feeling it might.

When we park, Lola turns to me and says, "Okay, Livie, this is the plan. Someone named Mr. Horne is about done with a meeting, and when he is done, he's going to personally walk you in. He said I should wait in the car."

"Lola, this is crazy!"

She literally pushes me out onto the sidewalk. I climb the steps and push the revolving glass door and immediately breathe in the cold, stale air of the bank. I just stand there, kind of frozen, until a woman asks me if I need help.

She leads me to Mr. Horne's office.

"You must be Olivia," he says, reaching out his hand.

"Yes. Thank you for doing this, I really appreciate it."

As he leads me downstairs to the boxes, I look around in awe. What if all these boxes contain secrets that, if revealed, could change people's lives?

When we get to 74C, he says, "Two minutes. And I can't leave you alone."

"Okay."

My hands shake as I open the small door to the safe-deposit box. Inside there are two files. One is from the adoption agency, and the other is unmarked. I decide to just open the one that pertains to me. Sure enough, there's all my information: what I weighed, what time I was born, etc. I scan down farther and *boom*, there it is, a name, typed with an actual typewriter, next to the words *birth mother*: Jane Armont, 1992. I let out a noise that is somewhere between a whine and a gasp.

"Are you all right?" Mr. Horne asks.

"Yes," I say, trying to pull myself together.

I put the file back and close the door. I pray he won't notice that there's a tiny earthquake happening all over my body. It's a wonder I can even walk. I'm not sure what exactly happens next, but eventually I make it upstairs and outside. When I get into the car, I can't speak. I'm still in shock.

"Just say the name," Lola says, pulling out of the parking space.

"Jane. Jane Armont."

"Oh dear, I think that's French. Hang on."

Lola pulls into a gas station and types the name into her phone. I look up at the palm trees and a few wispy clouds. I feel dizzy. I am now seeing through the eyes of a girl with a mother in the world. At least, the name of one.

"Nothing comes up, Livie. Just what looks like a very famous painter from Santa Fe who's about ninety years old."

She pulls back onto the road. As we drive, I think about the name Jane. It's a solid name, just like Rose—did I ex-

110

pect it to be Rose?—like she could be a nurse or a teacher, or maybe even a lawyer.

"You know, I've never gotten to call anyone *Mom*."

"It's overrated, dear, believe me. My mother is so obsessed with yoga and her bloody juice cleanses that we barely have any conversations anymore."

"But you did. You were close to her. And that relationship shaped the person you are."

"What are you, a shrink now? Listen, we'll find your mum, trust me. But I wouldn't have expectations. It's not going to be all Hallmark with you running off into the sunset with her."

"Well, maybe we can at least make cookies or something?"

Lola laughs and adjusts her scarf. "You could probably teach her a thing or two."

When she drops me off, Lola looks at me intently for what seems like a long time. "You know what? Mum or no mum, you will always be Olivia."

"Yeah. But right now Olivia feels like she just got hit by a truck."

"Well, you've got a date with Theo, right?"

"Yes! I'm supposed to meet him at seven forty-five." My heartbeat quickens and I look at my watch. I have a little over two hours.

"Nothing like a boy to get your mind off it. Jane Armont isn't going anywhere. So let's pause until we decide our next move. Deal?"

"Deal."

* * *

When I get inside, I take Rose's book out of my bag, close my eyes, and turn to another page. I open my eyes and see a drawing of an old man walking on a tightrope across a deep ravine. The recipe is FEARLESS FRICASSEE. From what I can tell, it's basically chicken stew. There's another note in the margin, this time in pencil:

9/8/68

Made for Mother and Eloise.
Mother pretty quiet.
Did she notice something?
Kurt was the elephant in the room.

In 1968, with her husband off to war and no sign of him returning, this woman put herself together and went to the store for chicken, red cabbage, and heavy cream. She made dinner for her reticent mother and the mysterious Eloise. . . . A housekeeper? A fling? It *was* the time of "free love." We studied that in school. Experimentation was everywhere. What else would her mother have noticed? What was it like living so close to the person who gave birth to you? Is there an unspoken bond, maybe even a tension, between mother and daughter that is vital to becoming a woman?

112

A few hours later, Bell comes home. He explains that the public defender is still gathering enough information to get Jeremy off. Bell is really stressed, so I toast some banana bread for him and spread butter on top, and he seems to be calmed by it as he chews. Again, I feel a rush of anger toward Jeremy. This is the last thing Bell needs. But I don't let on. Instead, I reassure him.

"Don't worry, Dad, he'll get out in no time."

"Yeah?" he asks me, like I'm the parent or something.

I give him my most serious look. "Yes," I say, trying desperately to believe it myself.

CHAPTER 14

When I was twelve, I basically had one friend. Her name was Jill, and she had a punk rock look but was shy if you tried to talk to her. Although I didn't know the word at the time, she was all about duality. One morning she didn't show up at school, and out of curiosity I went by her house on the way home. Not only was her whole family gone, there was a hippie couple moving in. They told me the family had moved to Wisconsin. When you're twelve, I guess you believe your friends will always be there. Well, I did. I couldn't fathom that she was gone, just like that. I sat on the curb for a while before getting up to leave. Everything—the sidewalk, the sky, the trees— looked a little different.

When I got to my front door and walked in, something shifted inside me. It was like the doorway was literally a threshold and womanhood was on the other side. I felt sick to my stomach and looked down at the spreading stain on my thrift-store sweatpants. Of course I had heard that one day this was going to happen, but now that it had, I felt frozen in time, waiting for someone to help, to explain what was going to happen from here on out. It's funny—health class explains stuff, but usually everyone is too busy joking around to really take in the facts. I knew I would get my period, and that would mean from then on I could get pregnant, but I didn't know much else.

Enrique came down the stairs, and his face was even more panic-stricken than mine. Gay men don't really like to deal with "female parts," and I could sense his apprehension, but he got it together. He brought me a roll of paper towels and said, "Hold on." Then he called Bell, who didn't seem to have much advice, and finally, he grabbed me and led me to Davida's door.

At that point, we didn't really know Davida more than to say a quick hello on the street. So the word *mortification* does not begin to explain how I felt. But that was how it happened: one of my gay dads taking my bleeding self to a total stranger next door. When Davida answered the door, it was like she read the entire situation in the blink of an eye. She completely took charge, pulled me inside, and sent Enrique home. For some reason—I found out later that my senses, strong to begin with, had become intensified—I remember all the smells in her house: patchouli, some kind of lavender oil, ripe tangerines in a bowl on her living room table. All the smells permeated my head, making me feel faint. Davida took me into the bathroom, taught me how to use a tampon, and gave me a large box of them. Then she suggested making me hot chocolate. I wanted to tell her I wasn't six years old, but Davida is the type of person who prefers impulse to common sense. I mean, technically I had just become a woman, and she was making me hot cocoa? But I went with it, and when we entered the kitchen I heard a few tiny little barks and saw, in his cage, an eight-week-old Hank, his cherubic face begging to be let out. Twenty minutes later I had completely forgotten about my period—all I wanted to do was play with Hank. He was the cutest chocolate Lab puppy I had ever seen in real life, almost as if he had jumped out of one of those cheesy greeting cards.

For a while, Hank replaced the loss of Jill. I would play with him every day for an hour after school. One time Davida had to leave, and Enrique came over and found me and Hank sleeping together on the couch. "You looked like two angels," he said. I remember counting the hours for school to be over so I could go home and play with the puppy. He was everything to me, and at the time, the idea of him not being around was the farthest thing from my thoughts.

Who had replaced Rose's loss? This Eloise person? Could Matthew and Kurt be replaced? Now, looking at the flyer for Hank's funeral, I suddenly feel helpless. I realize that as Hank had grown, I had taken him for granted. I even got mad at him and at times dreaded having to walk him. Now I would give my left arm to have him chew up my favorite slippers, or knock over my orange juice, or slobber on my jeans. I even miss the things that annoyed me about him. I hold the flyer to my chest and close my eyes.

It's not really a funeral. On the flyer it says *Drum Circle*, which unnerves me a little. But as long as it's for Hank, I have to go. I'm glad Theo's here with me, and that he was so understanding when I asked if we could go to this instead of going to Bean, after Davida stopped by with the flyer this morning. There are bowls of carrots and pretzels, and ginger ale. Theo picks up a carrot and smells it before taking a bite.

"Why do you smell your food?" I ask, giggling.

"I don't know. I'm kind of animalistic that way," Theo says. There are arrows drawn on paper, and we follow them out the back door.

Someone who calls himself a shaman runs Hank's "service." There's a fire pit in Davida's backyard, and we are all in a big circle. The shaman holds a stick that's supposed to represent Hank's spirit. As we pass it around we're supposed to give it good thoughts and energy. I am used to Davida and her New Age friends, but I think this is a little new to Theo. He seems really nervous. Still, at the end, when the shaman is going around hugging everyone, Theo whispers to me, "Be careful. Whatever you do, don't squeeze the shaman."

I silently laugh so hard I almost pee, and have to go

inside to the bathroom. When I come back, Theo is, in fact, squeezing the shaman.

"Soft?" I ask him.

"You don't even know."

We say our goodbyes and start heading down to Sunset. We get on the westbound bus and just sit in silence for a while. Suddenly exhausted, I lean my head against his shoulder and doze off. When we get to Santa Monica, we head out onto the pier and Theo buys me a twenty-five-cent poem from a guy on the street with an old typewriter. He types it on the spot. It says:

> *Pulling petals for you*
> *One by one*
> *Coming nearer*
> *To the sun*
> *We have only*
> *just begun*

I fold it twice and put it in my pocket. We sit with our legs dangling over the dock and watch some of the sailboats coming and going in the harbor.

"So," he says. "Third date starts at a dog funeral–drum circle. Definitely different."

I smile. "That's what you said you wanted. You seemed like you were really into it."

"I was trying not to laugh."

I punch him lightly on his shoulder.

"Thanks again for going with me," I say, growing serious.

"Liv, I know you loved that dog. One time you brought him into the restaurant and I ended up walking him, remember?"

"No."

Theo makes a noise and says, "You never really noticed me noticing you, did you?"

"Not really. But I noticed you when I saw that picture you taped to the wall."

"And then you added the road—that was so cool."

A boat horn goes off and some little kids start running down the dock.

"Did you ever get the bike?"

"No. My dad was supposed to send me money."

"Where does he live?"

"Vegas. He has a whole other family. It's like he just traded us in for a less screwed-up one."

"And your mom?"

"She's okay, I guess, but she doesn't have time for Timothy. She resents him for being retarded, like it's his fault."

"That's terrible."

"T's got a big heart, though. He just takes a lot of patience, which I never had until I started taking care of him. I can't really explain it, but it's kind of like nothing else matters, or everything else seems insignificant. But it's really nice hanging out with you. It feels like there's finally something else to . . . like. And I don't feel anything missing when I'm with you."

My stomach knots up, in a good way, but I turn the subject away from myself. "What is it about cycling for you? How did you get into it?"

"When I was little, I used to watch the races in the Valley. My dad took me, actually. Aside from liking the outfits"—he blushes, realizing that might sound weird—"I couldn't believe the power. I wanted to know what that felt like. Now, when I ride, the bike is like an eighteen-pound geared extension of *me*. You know? And I feel this surge of energy. It's a fine line between speed and catastrophe, safety and danger."

"So you like living on the edge?"

"I guess so."

Theo laces his fingers through mine, and we watch the sun fading behind the masts of the boats that stand tall as soldiers.

"I found out my mother's name," I say. "Yesterday." It feels so right to tell him this—and different from telling Lola.

"Wow. Did you always wonder about her, or just recently?"

"Well, I'd thought about it in a fleeting way, and in middle school a bunch, but after I met the psychic I felt like this seed was planted—I found this key, and it basically led me to discovering my mother's name."

"Do you know anything about her?"

"No, but I think she looks like Julie Andrews."

He laughs.

"Her name's Jane Armont. I'm getting used to saying it out loud."

"So what are you going to do now?" Theo asks.

"Find her."

"Well, Liv, I'm totally here if you need me."

We look out at some seagulls soaring through the darkening sky.

He leans over to kiss me, and even though he's not riding his bike and I'm not cooking, everything bad slips away.

CHAPTER 15

I step into the elevator, thinking about the doors I have opened since I first stepped through these, and it's starting to feel like a long time since I *didn't* believe in connections. Janice isn't in when I get to the office, so I take Rose's cookbook out and flip to somewhere near the middle. Next to an illustration of a hand chopping what looks like celery, it reads SIMPLE SAUCE.

In the margin, in Rose's delicate handwriting, is a list, with no date:

- *bring this sauce to Mother to cheer her up*
- *have someone fix the leak in the bathroom*
- *buy a new dress*
- *be happy*

My mind travels back to what Rose's life may have been like at that time. Husband still gone at war; sad, but with a will to change, to be in good spirits in spite of it all. Still, there are some doodles that look like teardrops, as if she was lingering on the last word: *happy.*

For the better part of the morning, I follow Rose's lead and make my own list. Between answering phone calls and sending out some faxes for Janice, it slowly forms.

- *find jane*
- *help bell*
- *go to paris (with theo?)*

I look at it and almost crumple it up. Nearly all the items are basically unattainable. What now?

Around lunchtime, Janice puts her hand on my shoulder and notices my list. I quickly cover it with some head shots that are on the desk.

"Paris, huh?"

How did she read it that quickly?

She gives me a sweet, encouraging look, so I feel like I have to explain.

"Remember my dream of going to Le Cordon Bleu?"

"Yes. Who's Jane?"

"Jane Armont. Just someone I—"

"Wait a second. Say that name again?"

"Jane Armont."

I know the *t* is probably silent, but I pronounce it

anyway. She looks like she might laugh or be sick, I can't tell which, and then the door opens. It's her one o'clock meeting, some writers for a pilot she's casting.

"Hold that thought," she says, and greets the guys, motioning them into her office.

Why did she freak out when I said that name?

During her meeting, I email the Contact tab on the website for Le Cordon Bleu.

To: paris@cordonbleu.edu
From: shecooks@jtuckercsa.com

Hi there—

My name is Olivia Reese and I'm almost seventeen years old.

I have been cooking since I was seven, and I actually create and serve a special in my dad's L.A. restaurant, FOOD, once a week. Anyway, my dream is to study at CB. I was wondering what the requirements are to apply, and if there are any scholarship opportunities.

Thanks,
Olivia

I downloaded the application a while ago, but it seemed so complicated I figured I'd just ask to get a straightforward answer. I hit Send and then Google my mother's name again to see if Lola missed anything, but it's still just the old painter woman in Santa Fe. I go to page three to see if something got buried, and sure enough, there's one item. It's all in French, but it clearly says Jane Armont, and the French word *propriétaire*, and something about Montreal. I try to uncover more, but there's nothing. It doesn't even seem to be related to the article that comes up. Is my mother in Canada? If that is the same Jane Armont, then she owns something in Montreal.

After Janice's meeting is over, she keeps her door closed for a while, then comes out with another weird look on her face.

"Red, why don't you come into my office?"

For some reason, I feel like this is it. She's going to fire me. I was wondering why she'd hired a teenager in the first place. Yes, I have done some of my own stuff while I've been here, but only if I'm done with everything she asked me to do. Should I have gone the extra mile and started cleaning the windows or something?

"So, I was going back and forth in my mind during the meeting."

"You're firing me."

She laughs, and I am momentarily appeased.

"No, you're not getting rid of me that easily. There was something I needed to confirm after they left, and after a few phone calls I did. You are not going to believe this."

Janice motions toward the other chair in her office, and I realize I'm still standing. I sit down slowly, half expecting the seat to explode. *What is going on?*

"When you mentioned that name, something clicked in my head. I had heard it before but couldn't place it. But then it came to me, in the middle of the meeting. And I confirmed it after—"

"What is it, Janice? Do you know her?"

"You could say that, yes."

I wonder why Janice doesn't ask me who it is, but it looks like she has already guessed.

"Oh my God." My fingers are trembling. I can feel my heart knocking on my rib cage. If she doesn't tell me the details right now, I'm going to spontaneously combust.

"You know that I go to Laguna Beach occasionally, right?"

"Yes."

"Well, there's a restaurant there, a little place called Five Feet. It's Jane's place."

I feel like I could scream. I open my mouth but nothing comes out except "Jane Armont?"

"Yes. She's the chef and owner of the place. I remember talking to her a few times. Her name is French, but she's American. She owned a place in Montreal before coming to Orange County."

Janice can see that I am shaking. She walks over and puts her hands on my arms, trying to hold me together.

"She's important to you?"

I nod. And then I can't hold it in any longer. "She's my mother."

"I thought so."

"Laguna is less than two hours from here," I say.

Janice walks slowly back around to her chair, a smile slowly forming on her face. "She has your hair. And your eyes. That's how I knew, really, from the minute I placed the name. But to be sure, I got in touch with the hostess, who's also the pastry chef. She told me Jane grew up right here, in Studio City."

It's a wonder my body is functioning, that I can even get air into my lungs. My mother is a chef in Laguna? Someone pinch me, please.

"Did she confirm that she gave a child up for adoption?"

"Well, I doubt Jane would give up something that personal, but trust me, Red, she's the spitting image of you. It's uncanny."

"Oh my God."

"I knew there was something familiar about you. Look what I have." Janice holds up a photo. "It's from my thirtieth birthday dinner, and you can't really see her clearly, but . . ."

She hands me the photograph. It's her and what looks like three young surfer guys. She's blowing out a candle. In the background there's the profile of a woman, kind of blurry, as if she was walking quickly through the frame. I can't really make out much of her face, but you can see her reddish hair. The exact same shade as mine.

I finally lose control of my breath, and I start heaving a little. Then my eyes churn out tears, rolling down my face one after the other.

*　*　*

Lola picks me up to go for coffee after work, and I am still holding the photograph in my hand.

"You're not going to believe this. Look."

I show her the picture and point to the red-haired blur.

"That's my mother. That's Jane Armont."

"What the bloody . . ."

"My boss knows her. She's known her for years. Isn't that crazy?"

"It's heavy bananas! What are you going to do?"

"Well, she told me to just chill out right now and not get too worked up about it. Yeah, right."

On the drive to the coffee shop Lola is unusually quiet. I know something is up, but I don't want to pressure her. It isn't until a few sips into our drinks that she starts talking.

"Livie, I'm afraid I have some news as well."

I'm not sure how much more I can take today, but I'm her friend, so I have to listen. "What is it?"

"Do you remember when I was worried about my mum cheating on Dad?"

"Yes, and it turned out she was seeing the gay acupuncturist."

"Right, well. She's been seeing loads and loads of people."

"What?"

"Because she's sick. The whole thing about the juice cleanses and the hydrotherapy and all of it, it's because she's sick. Very sick. And she wanted to try and cure herself in a natural way."

The word sits at the back of my throat, and somehow I say it out loud.

"Cancer?"

"Yes. I can't believe it. The irony of it all. Miss Health Conscious. Miss Yoga Seven Times a Week and spirulina smoothies and colonics and . . ."

In the three years that we've been best friends, I've never seen Lola cry. Now, her face contorts in an almost grotesque way, and she makes a slight moaning sound. I move my chair over to her and hold her as best I can. After a minute or two, she pulls herself together and says, "It's fine, I'm fine."

I move my seat back to where it was. I've lost the taste for my chai. For a while, we just sit there as the world goes on around us. Lola sighs and wipes at her eyes with the little napkin that came with her mocha. She looks like someone who's been clubbing all night, mascara running and hair a mess. I think about the fact that I could potentially be finding my mother while Lola is losing hers. Is this a law of the universe? Some sort of balancing out, where nothing is lost, just shuffled around?

We go to my house and I make Lola the Simple Sauce from Rose's cookbook and serve it with some chicken and vegetables. I try to bring up some of our funny history to lighten the mood. Like the time I tried to pretend I was British too, in front of a couple of boys, and how my accent was so bad but they fell for it. Or the time her taco fell apart and covered her sweater, right in front of Jin. It works for a little while, but then we start talking about what we're avoiding: the prognosis, the chemo, and the fact that her father is a mess.

I make her help me with the vegetables, and it seems to soothe her. "They say it's therapeutic, the repetitive motion of chopping," I tell her. "Like a painter getting lost in the colors, or a singer getting lulled by a melody."

"Well, I'll take any therapy I can get."

"Remember, every piece is a part of a whole."

We eat the meal at the kitchen table, listening to the distant cars and the chirping of the cicadas.

"I wonder if this life, our life, here in Silver Lake, is just a phase. If there are bigger things ahead for us."

"I do hope so," Lola says. "What about your brother?"

"They haven't gotten him out yet. I'm really angry at him for being so careless. It sounds harsh, but I think a few days in jail will be good for him."

After we're done, we share a cookie. No matter what crap is going on in life, a cookie will make it go away—just for a minute. The aroma encircles us in an invisible bubble of safety.

Lola and I say goodbye casually, knowing we will see each other tomorrow, but also knowing that nothing will ever be the same. We have no idea what will happen from now on. All we can do is try to get some sleep, and brace ourselves.

CHAPTER 16

My special tonight at FOOD is prosciutto-wrapped salmon. It's a simple dish that was inspired by Rose. She made a somewhat similar one and wrote only the name Eloise in the margin. I put the cookbook, open to that page, on the counter for inspiration.

I start to brush the salmon fillets with olive oil. Sometimes cooking makes my mind just go blank, but today it allows me to imagine . . .

Rose, coming in from the cold to her friend sitting at the kitchen table, smoking. It's 1968 and they don't really know it's bad for you, so it's somehow more glamorous. Eloise is dark-skinned, with almond eyes and cropped black hair, and she's wearing a cashmere

*sweater and a pencil skirt. They're only twenty. They've
known each other all their lives, and now they both
have husbands at war. The difference is, Eloise wasn't
in love with hers. He was just someone who was there,
and that's what you did in the sixties. So she married
at eighteen, without ever exploring her true sexuality,
which she is only understanding now. . . . In fact, she's
realizing she's in love with Rose, and probably always
has been.*

*Rose puts the ingredients on the table and they
exchange pleasantries, but there's something different
about Eloise. She's smoking rather slowly, and holding
her lips open a little longer after exhaling, watching
keenly as Rose pulls the items from the bag. . . .*

I sprinkle the fillets with fresh black pepper and wrap
each one delicately with a piece of prosciutto.

*By the time the meal is cooked and served, they've
each had two martinis. They start to feel like they're on
a heightened plane, like all the sorrow that has crowded
their world is disintegrating at the edges, leaving them
giddy and light-headed. They laugh like they're kids
again. When Rose goes to the bathroom, she thinks . . .*
Could it be? Why haven't I thought of that before?
The real reason Eloise's marriage is a wreck? But
Kurt, always there, an old friend, a warm body in the
night, the love of my life. I could never betray him.
Or could I?

One of the chefs comes up behind me and says, "Can't go wrong. You could wrap a shoe in prosciutto and it would taste good."

My special addition is a touch of Gorgonzola cheese sprinkled on top; by the time it gets to the table it's slightly melted. This dish is easy to bake, because when the prosciutto is crispy, you know the salmon's done. I place the three racks in the oven and start to clean up my station.

When Rose returns from the bathroom, there's music on. She can't remember the last time she played music in the house, and everything suddenly looks foreign to her, like she has walked into a movie about someone else's life. Eloise dances elegantly in the corner, a record in her hand, facing the phonograph. Rose walks slowly toward her, and when Eloise turns around she is frightened for a moment, but then calmed by Rose's smile. As if it was the most natural thing in the world, they kiss.

When the fillets come out of the oven I taste one, and since I barely have to chew the fish, I know I've done my job. I pair it with butternut squash and some sautéed spinach. One thing about spinach a lot of people don't know is if you salt the leaves before you sauté them, they become infused. There's nothing worse than bland spinach.

At about eight-thirty, Bell tells me there's a guest for me at table eight. I go out and see Theo, already eating my salmon. Sitting next to him is a boy who I assume is

133

Timothy. He looks like a plump version of Theo and has a scar above his left eye. He seems to be very contained at the moment, but he has an electric energy about him, as if his whole body is buzzing with nerves.

I sit down with them, and Theo compliments my dish by just pointing at it with his mouth full and rolling his eyes.

"Thanks." I turn toward Timothy, who smiles wildly at me.

"I love your fish," he says, his mouth also full.

"Thank you."

Theo reaches over and dabs at Timothy's mouth with his own napkin, and I melt inside. How lucky is Timothy to have Theo for a brother? I feel my face flush, and I excuse myself.

Later, from the kitchen window, I see Theo helping Timothy with his dessert, and again, the gesture is unbearably sweet. Bell comes up behind me and snaps me out of my trance.

"He's a good guy."

"Yes, he is. It's weird, every time I see him I feel more and more like I've known him forever."

Bell smiles at me. "That's a great feeling to have."

He's right, and I am happy, but it's not enough. I still need to find the missing piece, my secret ingredient. Is it my mother? I feel like finding my mom might solve everything, but I just can't do it yet. Because what if it doesn't? And as long as meeting her is in the future, like Theo said, anything is possible.

When I get home, I call Lola to check in. She sounds sad and frustrated, and we talk for an hour and a half, until we are pretty much asleep. I wonder if there's such a thing as an easy life and complete happiness. If Lola doesn't have it, I don't think anyone does.

CHAPTER 17

I'm getting ready to go over to Theo's place for the first time on Sunday morning when I hear a knock at the door, followed by a sneeze. I know it's a stranger because the knock sounds very formal. And anyway, at our house, people usually just walk in. I go downstairs and open the door. Standing there are two men in suits, one of them sweating slightly.

"Hello. Is Mr. Reese here?" says the unsweaty one.

"No, but I'm his daughter. Can I help with something?"

The men give each other a look, and I immediately translate it as: *not an issue for children.*

"Could you just leave this card with him and tell him to call me by the end of the day tomorrow? It's very important."

Ever since things started happening this summer, I've felt more fearless, and I find myself talking before I even decide what to say. "How much does he owe? For the mortgage."

"I'm afraid we can't discuss that with you."

"But that's what it's about, right?"

They don't say anything, which I take as a yes. I thank them as politely as possible and go inside to call Bell. He's not at the restaurant and doesn't answer his cell. I return the safe-deposit box key to its place inside Bell's desk, then go to his bedroom and put the man's card on his nightstand.

As I leave for Theo's, I feel pretty great, considering I may not even have a house to come home to soon. It's like, whenever I think about Theo, the world looks brighter, and there's a bounce in my step.

I find Theo's place and walk up to it. It's a small gray house off Sunset that could use a paint job. Theo answers the door, then leads me into his room, which is filled with cycling tools and posters from the Tour de France. I keep stealing looks at his legs—they're shaved, which is weird but cool, and they're definitely ripped. As he shows me his movie collection, his fish, and some old photos, I feel important, like not everyone gets let into Theo's world. He looks at me with his green eyes shining, like I'm worthy, maybe even beautiful. He kisses me again, and it's not like other boys' kisses. He's slow about it. It gives me this feeling of something growing out of me, like a flower opening toward the sun.

*   *   *

"The great thing is," Theo says, when he finally leads me back downstairs, "I found Timothy a caretaker, someone who specializes in his type of case. She's amazing. Her name is Hope. She's dropping him off now."

Watching Theo and how cute he is, I can see why his aunt encouraged him to try acting. His mouth forms an odd shape when he talks, and his eyes are super expressive. He's different, in a good way. But looks are only half the package.

A sweet-looking middle-aged lady brings Timothy inside and shakes Theo's hand. She isn't expecting me, and neither is Timothy, who starts fidgeting and looking everywhere but at me.

"T, this is Olivia—remember? The girl from the restaurant."

"You're really really really really pretty," Timothy says. His voice is loud and monotone. "You want to play checkers?"

"Sure," I say, thinking, *How hard could that be?*

As Theo repairs one of the tubes for his bike wheel, Timothy and I start playing checkers. Not knowing his exact intelligence level, I start to let him win. About halfway through the game, his expression, until now open and sweet, turns sour. The corners of his lips turn down and he squints a little. I can tell I've done something wrong.

"I can play checkers," Timothy says.

"I know," I say, feeling my cheeks flush, wanting to crawl under a rock.

Then, in a flat, low tone that doesn't even sound like his voice, Timothy says, "I'm not retarded."

A cloud comes over the room. Theo looks up from his bike wheel and says, "Easy, T. No one said you were retarded."

We start to play more, and all of a sudden Timothy's breathing really heavily. Then he picks up a checker piece and puts it in his mouth.

"See," he says, his words garbled, "I'm a wee tard."

I reach out to grab it, like he's a baby who might choke, which makes it worse, and he spits the checker piece right in my face. It hurts. He starts moaning a little, and rocking back and forth. I act like it's no big deal, because that's what you do in situations where it's totally a big deal. Theo comes over and quickly leads Timothy out of the room.

I'm not sure how long I'm alone, but it's long enough for the tears to completely dry on my face. When Theo comes back, he brings me tea. The cup has a lipstick mark from his mother on it, but it doesn't matter. Theo's gesture makes me want to curl up in his arms and stay there for days.

* * *

Later, Theo asks me if I will make something from what's in his kitchen.

"You have free rein," he says.

There's not much there. Lots of cereal and granola bars. I find a bag of black beans and two apples. I boil the beans with the apples and end up making burritos with (cringe) American cheese. He loves it, and Timothy, who has joined us at last, does too, the checkers incident seemingly forgotten. As I watch Theo with Timothy, Theo comes into focus. It's like when you see a house from the beginning of a long driveway get closer and closer as you drive up, and eventually you can actually see what's going on inside. Last year in the restaurant, Theo was always cool and smooth, like he hadn't a care in the world, but that was so far from the truth.

He seems to really appreciate everything in life, including Timothy, even though he's a lot of work. I can feel that he really likes me. I've never had this kind of intense interest from a boy before, unless you count Ryan Smith writing a notebook full of poems for me in fifth grade. I really don't know how to act. I never watch TV except for cooking shows, and not even movies, aside from Bell's favorites, and those are mainly black-and-white or involve singing and dancing, not making out. Except for some more contemporary books I've checked out from the library that have date scenes, I have no guide, no rules to live by. I suppose this is where having a mother, not just a nurturing Enrique, would come in handy, but in my utter naiveté, I just act like myself, the only way I know how, and it seems to work, especially in the kitchen. Bell's chef says that there is no one way to cook something. It's about intuition. I guess being with someone is the same way. When you spend time with someone, you have to trust yourself, give in to the moment. And for the first time, I'm beginning to trust myself, to feel worthy of the attention of a boy like Theo.

I'm starting to understand what Enrique described when he was talking about Bell. That unseen safety net, an underlying contentment that feels like a mild drug taking the edge off. Timothy gives me a big smile, as if he knows what I'm thinking about. Maybe he does. And suddenly, I feel like I have the strength to tell Bell and Enrique about Jane Armont.

But when I get home, my dads are running out the door.

"Come on! They're letting Jeremy out!"

We jump into our old Honda, and Enrique lets out a yip of victory.

"The public defender proved he didn't steal the truck," Bell says. "Jeremy signed papers, and the lawyer got ahold of them and found the guy who sold Jeremy the truck to confirm it. Jeremy still has to go to court, but he's free."

Both of my dads look so happy. I can't tell them about Jane now. Instead I sit, content, a slight smile lingering on the corners of my lips.

The precinct is eerily quiet. Bell goes up to sign some

documents, and Enrique puts his arm around me and squeezes.

Five minutes later, my brother comes out. He's mainly intact but looks tired and a little shaken. My smile diminishes.

We take him to a diner, where he scarfs down a three-egg omelet.

"And just 'cause I know it's what you're thinking, nothing happened," Jeremy says. "I was in a cell with some guy who set his wife on fire."

"That's comforting," Bell says.

"And I had to take a dump in front of him."

"Hey!" Enrique scolds.

Then Jeremy gets all serious. "Sorry, you guys. I was trying to help."

"I know," Enrique says. "We're just glad you're out."

I don't say anything, and I can't really eat. When Jeremy gets up to go to the bathroom, I follow him and stop him in the back hallway.

He turns to face me. "What is it, Ol?"

"You have to grow up, Jeremy," I blurt out. "You have to learn to think things through. The ice cream truck wasn't a good idea. It just made things worse." I feel myself gaining steam, like I might just slap him across the face.

"I know, dude. I screwed up."

"Yeah, well, that's all you ever do!" I want to keep yelling, but I really can't look at his face another second, so I turn around and go back to the table. A few minutes later, Jeremy comes back but doesn't look me in the eye.

"Listen, Jeremy," Bell says, "no more ice cream trucks, okay? The restaurant is picking up. We'll work everything out. In the meantime, just do your demo deal and work on your music."

"Shit!" Jeremy says, almost spitting out his last bite. "I was supposed to meet the songwriter chick. I'm so screwed."

All of a sudden, I go from the angriest I've ever been to sister mode. I guess that's how it is with family. You forgive them for things you'd never forgive anyone else for. And no matter how hurt I still feel, I want the best for Jeremy.

"Why don't I go with you, and we'll explain together?" I offer.

"That's a good idea," Bell says. "Enrique, you and I have to go deal with the bankers."

The waitress drops off our check, and Bell leaves some cash.

"Well, this has been real," Jeremy says.

"Nothing like an after-jail family get-together," Bell adds.

Enrique tousles my hair and says, "At least we know Ollie won't be breaking the law anytime soon."

If they only knew I already kind of did.

* * *

Jeremy and I take a bus to Manhattan Beach, where the "songwriter chick" has an office. Most of the way, we don't talk. Right before we get there, he turns to me with tears in his eyes.

"You're right, Ol. All I ever do is screw up. But this meeting, this track, it's going to pan out. I just know it. My heart's in it."

"Your heart has never been the problem. It's that pea brain." But I don't sound angry when I say it.

Jeremy laughs a little, wipes at his eyes, then grabs my shoulder.

"Forgive me?"

"I'll work on it," I say.

Even though I've never been there, the place seems very New York to me. It's a vast, open, industrial space with offices along the edges, which look more like hip living rooms. The songwriter's name is Penelope, but, as she tells us, everyone calls her Pen. She doesn't seem to care about Jeremy standing her up last night, and as he starts to explain the reason, I cut him off. She doesn't need to know he was in jail, right? Or maybe that would add to his rockstar allure. Jeremy looks at me gratefully, but I can tell he's kind of embarrassed that I'm saving the day.

After a few moments Pen tells Jeremy she has a song idea she wants to run by him, and looks at me like, *You can leave now*. I tell them I'll be just outside, in the "communal space," and make my exit. I sit down on a plastic red chair that looks like a giant tooth.

Through a large rectangular window, I see the ocean in the distance, the sun glistening off it, and a few random surfers riding the waves. After the Stingray Trauma, I've always treated the ocean like some sort of moving painting on a wall. Something to glance at. But now I actually contemplate it. I imagine myself on one of those surfers' boards, riding the curl of the wave. It must feel like flying.

A woman walks in with her arm around a girl who is obviously her daughter. Their stride is similar, and they have the same nose. The girl, although she's clearly excited, is acting like her mother is driving her crazy. For some reason, it reminds me of the day when the most popular girl in fifth grade, Jewel Eaton, came up and started talking to me. She even commented on my hand-me-down sweater. She told me we were destined to be friends. At the time, I didn't even know what *destined* meant, but I went with it. We hung out during recess, and at the end of the day, when we said goodbye, she said, "I think it's so cool that you have two dads. Can I come over sometime and meet them?"

Jewel lost interest in me pretty quickly. Perhaps she found another fad to cling on to. I was merely her project during "Child of Gay Parents" week. Anyway, even though I was sad that my friendship with Jewel was so short-lived, it was the first time I realized that different can be good. It wasn't until school that I understood having two dads is actually cool. Of course, there were some kids who teased me, and Jeremy—he got the worst of it. But I was lucky to learn at a young age that diversity is something to be celebrated. Even though I've never walked around with a rainbow flag or anything, I've always been proud of my two dads.

But now, looking at the girl and her mom waiting for her singing audition or whatever it is, I feel the absence I've been noticing lately even more acutely, like some tiny pinprick in my heart. My blood is pumping, but my breath keeps stopping short.

I can hear Jeremy and Pen working on the song, and it seems like they're on a roll, so I decide to take the bus back to Hollywood, and call Lola from a pay phone to see if she wants to hang out and can come pick me up. Turns out she's just glad to get out of the house. I wait on the corner of Hollywood and Vine, where there's a smattering of tourists, gift shops, and crazy street people. Everyone thinks Hollywood is some glamorous place where all your dreams come true, but the irony is, it's one of the saddest places in the world. It has a sense of desperation and tackiness that's almost tangible. The Hollywood Hills are different—besides going to a pool there with Enrique sometimes, I also once went to a party at one of Bell's friends' homes, and I stared at the view for hours—the sprawl of city lights and a small triangle of reflective ocean in the distance.

Lola pulls up and I get in. As we head east on the boulevard, I ask her how she is, but she doesn't want to talk about it anymore, so I tell her about Jeremy getting out. I look out the window, picturing Rose staring loss, tragedy, and war in the eye. Lola can sense I'm thinking about something.

"What is it, Livie?"

"Do you think I take risks?"

She gives me an odd look but doesn't say anything, which is a first for Lola.

"I mean, you're always the first one to, like, take risks and put yourself out there. But I feel like I'm too passive, you know?"

Lola presses the gas to get through a yellow light.

"See? When you see yellow, you speed up. I would have slowed down."

"Well, clearly this isn't about driving techniques. What are you getting at?"

"You might think I'm crazy, but the notes in the cookbook, they're coming more and more alive for me. This woman Rose, I think she was sleeping with her friend Eloise while their husbands were at war."

"Maybe you *have* gone a little mad."

"Anyway, the thing is, this woman was, like, super courageous, it seems. I keep delaying finding my mother because I want it to be perfect, which I know it probably won't be."

"You'll do it when you're ready. You're right to think it might not be so great. Your mother gave you up, and there was a reason for that. But just remember—even though she carries your genes, she doesn't define you."

"Then what does?" I ask her.

"Well, for one thing, the dishes you create. You're a master in that kitchen. It's like this other person comes out of you. I don't know . . . Super Chef."

I smile. "Yeah, I'm just wondering if I can carry some of that into my life."

"You are! You've got a job, you're dating a *boy*, and just the fact that you're *talking* about seeing Jane in Laguna—these are all good things."

Lola pulls up to the curb next to my house and puts her hand up for a high five.

"You're a star, Livie. And my best friend. Don't you forget it."

"You too," I say, and even though she's British, I give her a huge hug.

CHAPTER 18

Work goes by in a blur on Monday, because all I can think about is that I'm seeing Theo tonight. I watch the last minutes go by on Janice's retro clock, then take the bus directly to Theo's, counting the palm trees like I used to.

Theo is making Timothy SpaghettiOs when I walk into his kitchen, and his face turns bright red. "Liv, I can't believe I'm making something out of a can in front of you."

"Don't worry, I've had my share of Chef Boyardee. Me and him? We're like this." I twist my fingers together, and he smiles.

Theo tries to slip a napkin into Timothy's shirt, but Timothy grabs it away and does it himself. After his brother finishes, Theo smiles and says, "Okay, buddy, time for bed."

Timothy lets out a defiant yelp.

"Easy, T," Theo says, and puts away their plates. While Theo has his back to us, Timothy leers at me, like the game has changed. Maybe it has.

After Theo tucks Timothy in, we go into the den, and I tell him about Jeremy getting out of jail.

"What? You didn't even tell me he was *in* jail!"

"Well, it's not something that's easily woven into a conversation."

"I swear, being around you makes my own life seem easy. You've got a lot on your plate."

"I feel the same way about you. You've basically raised your brother. Oh, by the way, are you going to come back to screen-test? It's been weeks. I hope I didn't scare you away."

"No. I've been thinking about it. I'd still rather be a professional cyclist. But if I could make some money acting while I train, that would really help."

"So, what race do you want to win?"

"The one whose first prize is you," he says, kissing me lightly on the cheek.

I smile and pull away. "Theo?"

"Yeah?"

"I don't mean to pry, but where's your mother? I've been over three times and I've never seen her."

"Who knows. She's dating this guy in Manhattan Beach. Sometimes she leaves for weeks at a time. She's . . . well, let's just say she's not really parenting material."

"Well, at least you have a mom."

"I guess. There was this time, it's one of my earliest memories, when T was really small and I was about six. We rented a van and the whole family drove to the desert. This was before my dad ever took me to the races, and it was the first time I saw people road biking. I was mesmerized. The way they were all in sync and their legs were like machines. It was a group of them, maybe eight, and they were literally riding into the sunset, this giant red ball on the horizon. Later that afternoon, at a gas station, my dad bought me this." Theo picks up a miniature plastic bike from a cabinet by the TV. The rider's shirt once had writing on it, but it's faded away over time. Theo looks at it, his green eyes getting moist. He hands it to me and says, "I never lost it, as you can see. I remember being in the tent, and T had fallen asleep. I could hear my parents giggling in the next tent over, and I just felt like I was in the right place, like everything was meant to be."

We sit down on the couch, and I rest my hand on his forearm.

"That was the last time I felt that way," Theo says, running his fingers down my neck, "until now."

"Really?" I ask.

"Yes."

"This may sound weird, but all I want to do right now is put my head on your shoulder and watch a movie. Can we do that?"

"That can be arranged," Theo says, beaming his beautiful smile.

We end up watching a super-old cycling film called *Breaking Away*. My emotions are all over the place, so I end up laughing and crying, sometimes in the same scene. When it's over, he leads me into his bedroom and we start kissing. I'm not sure how my clothes come off, but they do, and his body is the warmest thing I've ever felt. I don't think about how we haven't discussed whether we are boyfriend and girlfriend. His skin's so soft that I run my hands all over it and it makes no sound. With the other boys I've kissed, I never came close to the connection I'm feeling right now. I'm not sure if it's because of everything that's going on, but I'm holding on to Theo like he's the only buoy in a vast, angry ocean. He's the one who first told me anything is possible, and I'm starting to really believe him.

Staring at me when I wake up is a poster from the Tour de France, and for a split second I think, *Yes, I'm here, in Paris*, but then I see Theo's cute cycling shoes and realize I'm in his bedroom. I hadn't planned on spending the night, but I do remember calling Bell and telling him I was staying at Lola's.

Theo is sleeping like a baby. Instead of waking him, I kiss him lightly on my favorite place, under his ear, and then slip out the side door and head back home to change for work.

Walking down Sunset, I think about the fact that I'm a woman now, in the full sense of the word. It's weird, it didn't seem like that big of a deal to me. It was so easy, and he was so gentle. He took his time and kept asking me if it hurt. It did a little, at first, but something told me it would get better, and it did. A lot better. It just felt right, like the natural progression of things.

I'm not a virgin, and my mother is in Laguna Beach. It's a free country, and as long as I'm prepared for any possible outcome, I can find her. It's time to stop putting it off and take control.

CHAPTER 19

I phone Lola during my lunch break and tell her that I'm ready. She offers to take me, but she understands when I say I want to go with Theo. She wants to be with her mom, anyway.

Over the next week, Jeremy works day and night with Pen and with this new band for his big showcase at Largo. Lola spends a lot of time taking her mother to and from her first set of chemo treatments. I try to get more out of Janice about my mother, but she's too busy, and not knowing what I'm planning for the weekend, isn't aware of the urgency of the situation. I talk to Theo on the phone every night and brainstorm on how we're going to get to Laguna. Miraculously, when I get home on Friday he's outside my house, on a motorcycle.

"Hey, Liv. I borrowed it from my uncle! Told him it was an emergency. We're going to Laguna."

I can feel my heartbeat start to pick up, like someone stuck a nickel into my slot.

"Really?" I say, as if I haven't been planning this all week.

He nods like a little kid, and right then I know that no one and nothing is going to stop me. My dads wouldn't want me to go without telling them, never mind on a motorcycle, but it's just something I have to do.

I go inside and put on a Windbreaker, and when I come back out, Theo is smiling, holding out my helmet. Next thing I know we're speeding south on the 405 freeway, the tires gripping the road, my arms wrapped tightly around Theo's chest.

Eventually we veer off the freeway and snake down the canyon toward Laguna. At the bottom of the ravine, there's a giant beach shaped like a half-moon and a park behind it with perfectly green grass, and there are people of all ages on bikes, on Rollerblades, carrying surfboards, and having picnics.

"Wow, it's like central casting for a beach town."

Theo laughs. "You got it."

We park and get ices, and Theo asks an older guy where Five Feet is, and the guy points behind us and says, "Two blocks down and two blocks to the right."

We start moving, and I turn to Theo. "Can I go alone?"

"Of course, Liv. You see that seawall over there? That's where I'll be."

At the top of the block I see a small orange awning halfway down the street, but no sign, and three steps to the front door. When I get there, I notice two tables in both of the front windows, a single pink flower on each. I put my hands up to peer inside and realize they're shaking.

There's an older man cleaning the floor, and a large gray dog that looks really bored. No sign of Jane. The walls are painted butter-yellow and hung with black-and-white pictures of abstract landscapes along with four antique sconces. Janice was right about the size of the place; there are only five tables. Just beyond the dining area is a small chestnut-colored bar with four stools and the kitchen on the other side. If I could ever imagine myself running a place, it would look something like this.

The kitchen door next to the bar swings open, and a woman comes out. Before I can see if it's her, I quickly slide out of view. My heart is beating, like, a thousand times per second. If someone had told me a month ago that I would be in Laguna playing hide-and-seek with my birth mother, I would have had them committed. But here I am, frozen, my back against the wall. If she sees me, how do I explain?

After a few minutes, the man who was mopping the floor comes out with his bucket. Instead of looking at me questioningly—what would I be doing there?—he just smiles and nods. I do the same and cross the small porch to the steps. I look at him once more, and something in his eyes is familiar. I swear I've seen him somewhere. He has white hair and a few days' growth of beard, and he's wearing a small silver necklace in the shape of a sailboat. I wonder what his story is. Probably something that pales next to the one I could create for him. Could he have had another life, like Kurt did at war? He is old enough to have lived through a war, lost a child. He gives me another warm glance and lets me pass, almost as if I were expected there.

When I get back to Theo, he looks at me expectantly.

"I can't do it," I tell him. "Not now. But I saw the place, and her, I think. It's so cool, only five tables. I don't know, I need more time to think about what I'm going to say, you know?"

"I get it, Liv. She's not going anywhere. We can do this anytime. But we'll have to leave soon. I promised my uncle I'd have the bike back to him by six. We do have a little time, though. Let's not think about anything, and just walk. Does that sound cool?"

He starts to lead me down the path that snakes along the coastline.

"Not sure if I can just not think about it," I say.

"Well, you can try."

I do try, but there are so many thoughts swimming around in my head. *What am I doing? What if my mother doesn't care? She obviously didn't to begin with. Why would she now? I have to go back.*

Eventually, though, the walk does clear my head, and on the way home to Silver Lake, I hold on to Theo even tighter.

CHAPTER 20

I obsess about Laguna all Saturday, and my special at FOOD that night is definitely not one of my best. On Sunday, I make zucchini bread and take it to Lola's house. It's pretty much the only thing that isn't making Lola's mom nauseated at the moment. I feel extremely uncomfortable and don't know what to say most of the time, but Lola seems grateful I'm there.

Monday morning, I call Lola and ask her if she can take me to work, and she tells me she'll be there in twenty minutes. As I make breakfast, I think about Rose and Eloise. How brave they might have been. Like two impossible ships coming together in the night. But then I imagine Kurt coming back from war unexpectedly. . . .

By this time, Eloise has basically moved in. She's been turning Rose on to women's lib, brought her a magazine with Gloria Steinem on the cover. Rose knows it can't possibly work, but strangely, it feels right. She also knows that they've now drawn a line that is permanent, and nothing will ever be the same between them. But for the first time in over a year, she has gone a whole day without thinking about the baby she lost. She sits at the kitchen table while Eloise is sleeping. It's late in the morning. Without warning, the door opens and there he is, looking tan and weathered, a duffel bag over his shoulder . . . Kurt. Smiling that unmistakable smile . . .

Lola honks and startles me out of my daze. As she takes me to work, she tells me she has a plan.

"I know you went with Theo and just scoped it out, but I think we should go, the two of us, next weekend. I told my mother and she's fine about it. She even gave me her credit card. We can stay at the Surf and Sand Resort and order room service. And if you want, we'll just go to her restaurant for dinner. That way you can see her without looking suspicious, right?"

"That actually sounds like a great idea."

"See, that's why I'm tops." Lola pulls up to my building and adds, "You've got to tell your dads, though. That you're going, I mean."

"I know. Meet me at my house after work today?"

"Brilliant."

"Hey, have I told you lately that you totally rock my world?"

"No, but you're welcome to now."

"You totally rock my world."

"As you do mine, Livie. Call me every five minutes."

As the day goes by, Lola's plan sinks in. I look at the cookbook just once and notice a recipe for a fricassee. So after work, I decide to get ingredients for it. A fricassee can be made with pretty much anything as long as you stew it, but it's usually made with white meat. I decide to follow Rose's traditional recipe, which calls for chicken and vegetables stewed in gravy.

No one is home when I get there, and I put on some mellow music and start chopping the vegetables. My nerves begin to calm, and I look at the single word that is, once again, written in the margin of the cookbook.

Eloise.

It's as if Rose was about to write something but then thought it might be incriminating. . . .

Kurt drops his bags and opens his arms, and for a second Rose thinks everything will be normal again. The hug lasts several minutes, and she doesn't even think about Eloise sleeping upstairs. Kurt explains the loophole that got him home as if he had won the lottery. Then his face goes dark and he shakes his head, tells Rose there's stuff he's seen, things he will never mention. When he notices the ashtray on the counter, with four of Eloise's cigarette butts in it, his face goes even darker and his brow furrows, like a child who doesn't understand. . . .

I pound the chicken and put it in the broiler. We're out of white onions, so I use shallots. Then I start on the carrots. . . .

Rose dumps the ashes in the trash and says, "Eloise is here; she stayed the night." It feels so strange to hear herself speak the words. She hugs Kurt again, tight, this time wondering how in the world she's going to get out of this predicament, and in walks Eloise in a lavender nightgown, her hair unruly, a willowy presence in the otherwise heavy air. She smiles, but there is agony in her eyes. They have never talked about Kurt coming back. They have no plan for how to even behave. Eloise acts as normal as possible and pours herself a cup of coffee. The next moment is brutal. None of them says a word. Finally, Kurt goes into the bedroom and Rose follows. Luckily, Eloise's things are in the spare room, but she's just left their bed. Will he be able to smell her?

I sauté the shallots, retrieve the chicken, and put it all in the wok. The recipe calls for a large saucepan, but if they'd had woks back then, that's what they would have used. The kitchen smells really good. I start to boil water and measure the rice. . . .

They are in there for a long time, and Eloise can only hear muffled voices. She goes into the spare bedroom and gathers her things. She can't get her toiletries, at least not right now. She goes outside and climbs into her pale blue T-Bird. She drives away and tries not to look back.

Lola arrives in a flurry, and we sit down at the table. The fricassee is pretty darn good. As we eat it, I tell her more about my musings regarding Eloise. Lola seems intrigued but also looks at me a little funny.

"I just picture these two strong girls, against all odds, taking the risk of their lives," I say a bit defensively.

"Well, Livie, I wouldn't get too carried away. After all, Eloise could've been a dog."

In my dream, Jane Armont is wearing a flowing blue dress. She is preparing dinner for a group of children. She gathers them all around a large table and starts serving them spaghetti. I come to the door with Hank by my side. There is no room at the table. I try to speak, but it sounds more like moaning, and she just shakes her head slowly.

When I wake up, it's two a.m. and my forehead is sweaty. I go to the bathroom to get a towel and notice that the door to the Dads' room is open and Bell is not inside. Where would he be at two in the morning? I wash my face, then tiptoe downstairs. He's in the big blue chair, just sitting there.

"Dad, are you okay?"

He looks over at me, and the only way I can describe his face is deflated.

"Are we losing the restaurant *and* the house?" I ask.

"No. Well, I don't think so. But something has to happen."

"Well, what about all your friends? People love you. Everyone loves you. As a matter of fact, I've never met anyone who didn't love you."

"What about Ms. Birnbaum?"

He's right. My fourth-grade teacher was a homophobic nightmare.

"Okay, but that's it."

"Pretty good track record?"

"Yes. Maybe everyone can chip in or something. Like at the end of *It's a Wonderful Life*."

"Ah, I'm not exactly Jimmy Stewart. Am I at the end of my movie?"

I don't have the heart to inquire about the card from the bank people, and I don't know if Bell wants the answer to this question to be yes or no, so I decide to go ahead and distract him with my own news.

"Well, something happened to me, and I guess I have no one to tell. I mean, there's Lola, but her mom has cancer, and she's already been so great helping me with . . . other stuff, so there hasn't been a right time."

"Oh, Ollie, that's horrible. How is she holding up?"

"Well, you know Lola."

"Yes, I do. She'll be okay. But it won't be easy." Then Bell's thoughts seem to turn back to our family. "Maybe we should run away and join the circus."

"We wouldn't have to audition. We could just say, 'Look at our life!'"

Bell laughs, and the sound of it gives me comfort.

I look him right in the eye and say, "Theo and I, well, we . . . I know it's supposed to be a big deal, but it wasn't for me."

"You mean . . ."

"Yes."

I know it's weird to tell your father that you're not a virgin, but what can I say? Bell is my father, but as I mentioned, he's also like a friend.

He bends over and hugs me, and I can tell he's swallowing his emotion.

"I hope those are happy tears," I say.

"I'm happy for you."

"Thanks."

"Well, I assume you used . . ."

"Protection? *Yes*, Dad. Of course."

"Whew."

I take him into the kitchen and fix him some toast with butter and sprinkled sea salt, placing it on a paper towel in front of him, along with some of the leftover fricassee I made for Lola. He eats it like it's his last meal.

"So, Jeremy's big showcase is tomorrow—well, technically tonight," I say.

"I know. I've got some of the staff going."

Light starts coming in from the kitchen window, and it gives the room a magical, predawn glow.

I go back upstairs and lie down. I wonder if Rose told her mother when she first did it. Was Kurt her only one? When we finished, Theo fell asleep against me, and he made this soft purring noise, and I nestled against him. It was crazy adorable. What I love about Theo is he's such a gentleman. Which is how I picture Kurt . . .

Rose comes out of the bedroom and can tell Eloise is gone. She tells Kurt that Eloise is troubled, has been staying for a while. She feels okay about omitting some of the truth. They found some sort of domestic bliss, but they weren't really lovers. Eloise wanted more; Rose just couldn't do it. Yes, there was the kiss after dinner, but from then on they just held each other through the nights. How else could they get through? Kurt knows something was a little strange, but he is so grateful to be home, he doesn't second-guess anything. At least not right away . . .

Does everyone carry these kinds of secrets? I try to imagine the depth of Jane Armont's secret. Having a child out in the world but never knowing what she has become.

I send a secret prayer out into the universe for my dads, for Jeremy, for Lola's mother, for all of us. All we can do is keep going and hope for the best.

CHAPTER 21

The next day at work, after organizing a bunch of files for Janice, I hear a familiar *bing* from my screen. I stop what I'm doing and see that there's an email from Le Cordon Bleu:

From: paris@cordonbleu.edu
To: shecooks@jtuckercsa.com

Bonjour!

You have requested information on Le Cordon Bleu Paris. Many thanks for your interest. We are one of the leading schools dedicated to culinary excellence.

Our professional training consists of three certificates—Basic, Intermediate, and Superior—in Cuisine and in Pâtisserie. Each certificate is eleven weeks long. Students may choose to study both Cuisine and Pâtisserie, to be awarded the Grand Diplôme Le Cordon Bleu, or they can choose one path of Cuisine or Pâtisserie, which culminates in the Diplôme de Cuisine or the Diplôme de Pâtisserie. Students may also choose to enroll per individual certificate. We run otherwise four sessions every year; training can start at any of these sessions.

Please find attached Le Cordon Bleu Paris course details, schedule of courses, price lists, and application forms. Let me know if you are interested in our professional training.

Sincerely,
Laini Montreau
Service Clientele
Le Cordon Bleu

Just reading it makes my heart race. I'm not seeing Theo until Thursday, as he said he's busy today and tomorrow, and I'm not going to Laguna with Lola until Saturday. So it's nice to have something else to think about. I print the email, fold it, and slide it into my bag.

I notice the cookbook and wonder if there are any notes I haven't read yet. I flip through, seeing some of the notes I've already read, dishes I've already made. Then, next to a drawing of someone pulling a star down from the sky, I read DARE TO DIP. Below is a recipe for what looks like a Tex-Mex dip. Rose has written only one thing in the margin:

Kurt would have loved this.

I can feel my pulse in my throat. There's no date. Was this before or after he came back from the war? The dip looks a little rich, but maybe I could do a variation on it. After all, isn't that what we're here for? We are given ingredients, and it's up to us to spin them, make them sing. There's no single way to cook something. It's about intuition, and knowing that even the most unexpected flavors sometimes go together.

On my way home, I decide to get the ingredients for Dare to Dip and make it for Theo. I know he's busy, but he's got to eat, right? I can just surprise him and drop it off. The small market on Vermont has everything except jalapeños, but the guy at the taco truck at the bottom of our street gives me some for free. He asks me where Hank is. I tell him I'm not sure. The man, along with everyone in our neighborhood, loved that dog. How can I tell them? Are some things better left unsaid? Did it really matter if Rose didn't tell Kurt everything?

I get home and start to boil the black beans immediately. The recipe calls for a paste, which I've never really made before, but how hard can it be? I peel the onions and start to halve, then quarter them. . . .

Rose doesn't like secrets. She's never had any at all, until Eloise. Even losing the baby, everybody knew about that. She wasn't ashamed about it, just sad. Three weeks go by and nothing from Eloise. One morning Rose is cleaning the bathroom and hears something break on the floor. At once, the smell fills her chest with emotion: she has broken a small bottle of Eloise's perfume. Rose thought she had gotten rid of everything, every sign of her, which felt like a betrayal, but how could she not? As it turns out, she is not one of those women. She is, and always will be, in love with Kurt. Still, she stops to smell it for a little while. Until her mother, who has let herself in, surprises Rose by walking up to the threshold of the bathroom door.

The paste comes out well. I add minced garlic. I place the tomatoes in a big colander and run water over them. Then I get the large knife and start to cube them. . . .

Rose looks up at her mother in her demure navy waistcoat and feels like a child caught doing something she shouldn't have been doing. Her mother is the only one who knew anything. About three days after the kiss, all three of them had dinner together. Eloise was being her usual self, nonchalant yet daring, brushing one of her stockinged feet along Rose's calf under the table. Rose found it incredibly liberating and giggled like a schoolgirl. Her mother knew something was off. Her generation was so rigid. All her friends had grandchildren, and after Rose losing the baby, her mother resented her, but only subtly, which is the worst way. But homosexuality? Forbidden. Her mother pitied her, and also felt sorry for herself. . . .

What I would give to know that feeling, that bond between mother and daughter, no matter how troubling. When Jane looks at me this weekend, will she immediately be tuned into my feelings, automatically see through me?

I start to layer everything in the casserole dish: the black bean paste, onions, tomatoes, sour cream. I use real avocado instead of guacamole. Now comes the laborious part: grating three kinds of cheeses. . . .

Rose stands up and says, "It's not what you think, Mother." Her mother doesn't look convinced, and says, "Well, I brought you some rolls." Rose doesn't like her mother's cinnamon rolls, hasn't since she was a kid. But the fact that her mother has brought them is touching. And Kurt, of course, will devour them. There is nothing that man wouldn't eat. Rose thanks her mother and, with her eyes, asks her to leave. She needs to pick up these pieces herself.

Would Jane have brought me rolls? If and when I get married, will she help me pick out a dress? I spread all the cheese in layers, substituting Monterey Jack for mozzarella, as that's what we have in the fridge. I preheat the oven and start dicing the jalapeños.

Sure enough, that night Kurt eats two of the cinnamon rolls. He has lost weight in Vietnam, so Rose is happy to see him filling up. The night before, Kurt woke up several times from terrible dreams, and Rose doesn't even want to know what they are, the things he's done and seen. She can only imagine. The important thing is that he's home now, and he's safe. After watching The Ed Sullivan Show, *they go to bed, and Kurt takes his time with her, kissing her cheek, her neck, her collarbone. . . .*

When the dip comes out of the oven, I put a towel underneath it and walk over to Theo's. I must look a little odd, walking the streets with a sizzling dip, but there are stranger sights to be seen in Silver Lake.

By the time I get there, the cheese is perfectly warm and gooey. I am praying Theo has tortilla chips, or even pita bread we can bake. Otherwise we'll be eating this dip with a spoon. Hope is in the front yard with Timothy, who smiles when he sees me. But then he gets a panicked look on his face. I look up at the house. Just beyond Timothy, through the kitchen window, I see the last thing in the world I am expecting—Theo, dancing with a girl. His arm on the small of her back, her hair in a high ponytail.

My body seems to be stuck in one position, and I stop breathing. I feel like I might lose my balance. Timothy makes a noise that sounds like he's repeating the word *no* over and over. The dip falls from my hands and crashes onto the driveway. I look down at it, briefly wondering how something so perfect can become so ruined in the blink of an eye. Timothy's still shaking his head, and Hope is looking at the ruined dip, her hands over her mouth. She starts to say something, but I don't hear her. I turn around and run.

On my way home, I consider going back to confront him. I wish I could just barge in there and start yelling, but that's not my style. Now I'm even more thankful I'm going to Laguna in two days. Half of me knows that finding my mother trumps wallowing in self-pity over my first love cheating on me. Still, I feel like my heart has exploded, and the other half of me wants to curl up into a ball and cry for hours. Rose would never do that, would she? She would forge on, make her next recipe, against all odds. Maybe there's an explanation, but it certainly looked like what I thought it was. I tell myself to set it aside, which is easier said than done. But I have no choice because tonight is about Jeremy.

Largo is packed with a lot of young men in suits and sport coats, which doesn't match the saloonish vibe of the place. Bell and I have a small table right off the side of the stage. Down-tempo house music plays to warm things up. Not my first choice, but it's calming me after what I just saw. Bell can tell I'm hurt.

"Ollie, what is it?"

"Nothing, Dad."

If I talk about it, I'll cry. I have to pretend it didn't happen.

"I heard it's impossible to get a gig here," I whisper to Bell. "He's always wanted to."

Lola appears at the table and says, "Nothing is impossible. Hi, Mr. Reese."

"Oh, hi, Lola!" Bell kisses her hand.

For the next few minutes, as the place fills up, Bell and Lola talk and gesture, getting along as they usually do, but I'm not really listening to them. I am picturing the girl in Theo's kitchen. Blond, of course. I unclench my fists and try to breathe deeply.

Jeremy isn't introduced, but the lights go completely black, and you can hear the first notes of his song "Broken." Everyone thinks it has these deep meanings, but it's just about the time he broke his arm. It sounds like some of the lyrics have changed, though, and he's really singing the story, and even though I'm still a little mad at him, of course I'm rooting for him anyway. I truly am swept up and completely moved by his performance.

Lola and Bell hoot and holler, and I just shake my head in wonder and clap like crazy. There's a lot of whispering going on, but when Jeremy starts his second song it goes completely quiet again. This must be the song he wrote with Pen, because I can see her beaming across the room. It's more pop than Jeremy usually is, but it sounds really great.

By the fifth song, the place is completely packed, and you could hear a pin drop. I am starting to believe this is real, that Jeremy may have a life doing this. I know I sound like Davida, but the whole room has this energy to it, like everyone can sense history is happening, that this night will be reminisced about for years to come. I look over at Bell, who seems to be feeling it too. Lola has her eyes closed and looks serene, which I've never witnessed before. I can see Enrique, who is sitting in the back with Luisa since we ran out of chairs at our table. He's smiling from ear to ear.

Before his last song, Jeremy says, "This one's about being in jail. Thanks for coming."

Bell and I look at each other and roll our eyes. The song, called "Inside," is heartbreakingly beautiful and sad. It's not so much about being in jail as about being at the end of one's proverbial rope. Everyone has been there. I notice a few people dab at their eyes. Jeremy's voice sounds better than I ever remember it sounding. I hear the psychic saying *He will soar*. I wish with all my might that she's right. She seems to have been right about a lot of things. The one thing she never mentioned was my fear of the ocean, which has been weighing on my mind lately. I've always thought of that incident as having had such a hand in shaping my reserved nature. If I want to break out of that, to be more adventurous, less passive, maybe I need to face my fear. Plus, it wouldn't be a bad idea, given that I'm about to go back to Laguna, a place so focused on the ocean that the town name includes the word *beach*.

Bell takes off early to make sure FOOD is running smoothly, and Enrique goes with him. Lola and I wait for

Jeremy, who's doing something he usually hates to do: schmoozing. When he finally makes it over to our table, he gives me a long hug.

"Dude, what did you think?"

"I'm at a loss."

"Poignant!" Lola says.

"Thanks, Lo. You taking good care of my sis?"

"Trying."

"Jeremy. How did you just, like, become a rock star overnight?" I ask.

"Well, jail helped."

"Right?" Lola says, as if she knows all about the big house.

"Anyway, Mr. Man over there says he thinks we have two possible deals . . . bidding war or some crap like that."

I jump up and down a little. "No way!"

"I know! Hey, where are the Dads?"

"They had to go back to FOOD. They stayed for the whole thing and were smiling the entire time. They loved it." I notice everyone looking over at us. "You should mingle."

"I have to go pick up my mum," Lola says, then turns to me. "See you tomorrow?"

"Yes. Please tell her I say hi, okay?"

"Will do. She loved the zucchini bread you made her."

As Lola heads out and Jeremy goes back to talk up the suits, I sit down and take a large sip of juice. I look at the empty stage, still flooded with red and yellow lights, and I can't help but think about how much more is out there for Jeremy and me. More than this room, this neighborhood, this city. It's as if everything up until now has just been flour, yeast, and eggs, the basic foundation, and now it's time to see if we'll rise.

CHAPTER 22

"Laguna?"

I'm getting the feeling that Bell is not exactly receptive to the idea, seeing as he's pacing around the kitchen.

"Lola needs to get away for a couple days. She's been working so hard, caring for her mom. She needs something for herself." I realize as I say this that it's true and make a mental note to follow through on it. "Her aunt will be here taking over soon, but she'll still have a lot to deal with."

Bell runs his fingers through his hair, never a good sign.

"Dad, it's fifty miles away. No big deal."

He takes a minute or two and then looks at me like I'm a lost cause. He throws his arms up and says, "Okay, okay. Go, then. I know you can take care of yourself." He looks out the window like he's trying to make out something in the distance. Then he turns back and says, "Here," handing me some cash. "Why don't you make the special tonight since you won't be here over the weekend?"

I don't tell Bell about Jane Armont, and I wonder if I really would have gone through with it that day even if Jeremy hadn't been put in jail. That bridge may be crossed later. Instead I give him a tight hug and say, "Sure. Thanks, Dad. I can get the ingredients after work. I'll get something that won't need to be cooked."

Lola picks me up from the office, and we head to the farmers' market. She looks different, like someone punctured her and she lost a little air. I can see the toll everything's taking on her.

"Isn't it a bit ironic, you gaining a mother and me losing one?"

"Your mother's going to get better. And I'm not going to let mine know who I am until I feel it out, as planned. I don't want to, like, disrupt her life."

"Well, she disrupted yours."

"I guess you could say that."

The farmers' market is super crowded. A few people bump into me as they walk past. Aside from being a place for people to check each other out, it's where you can buy local. I taste a sample of a watermelon and decide on a salad. I buy two ripe watermelons, four bags of arugula, pumpkin seeds, and some special soft feta cheese.

"I just hope—I mean—sometimes you get a taste of something and it isn't enough," Lola says.

"Well, I know that this Jane Armont person isn't going to drop everything and start mothering me, but I still need to see her."

"I know, just be careful. It'll be great whatever happens—don't worry about it."

Lola helps me bring the stuff over to FOOD, and as she's leaving, I grab her arm and say, "Sometimes you call me a star. Well, *you're* the star. You can't lose that light you give out, that shine you put on the world. It needs Lola, the world needs Lola."

She starts to get teary, but when Jeremy comes up on his bike, she composes herself.

"Thanks," she says, touching my arm, and walks away.

Jeremy hops off his bike. "Did I interrupt something?"

"Long story. What's going on?"

His face lights up, and I know he got a record deal. My brother got a record contract.

"Dude, it was a bidding war. Can you even deal? They want the cowrite with the cougar to be the single, but I don't really care anymore. I'll get behind a machine if it means I get a colossal advance and the chance to be heard." He shakes the hair out of his face. "I know I've been a nightmare up until now. But this is it, Ol, this is my calling. By the way, I saw your Biker Boy. He came to my place looking for you."

"He did?"

"He seemed kind of aggro."

I don't want to go into the whole Theo thing with Jeremy, so I give him a hug and say, "I gotta go prep. I'm so happy for you."

"Yeah, well, nothing's signed yet, but it's all supposedly happening."

"As much as I'm still annoyed with you, you deserve it."

"Thanks, Ol. See you later."

For my special, I slice a large thin rectangle of watermelon and put it on the bottom of the plate, then crumble feta on top. . . .

Rose hasn't seen her for months, but she knows Eloise got arrested during a Women's Liberation demonstration. She sees Eloise's picture in the paper, and feels her chest swell with pride. Rose is bold, but she would never have gotten arrested. It's a warm Saturday, and Rose is shopping with her mother. They're going to make Welsh rarebit, Kurt's favorite. Her mother is in great spirits, as Rose's bump is beginning to show. When people ask, her mother takes over the conversation as if she is having the baby herself. Rose doesn't mind. She's happy, and knows it's what everyone wants.

If I ever get pregnant, will Jane be there to give me pointers? Will she ever know that she's a grandmother? I add a line of arugula, and a sprinkling of pumpkin seeds for crunch. Then I start cutting lemons for the dressing. . . .

Except Eloise. And there she is, standing by the melons, looking beautiful as ever, but when she gets closer, Rose notices something has drained from her eyes; they've lost their shine. Rose's mother immediately excuses herself, and Rose is grateful. They stare at each other and smile. Eloise points to Rose's bump and congratulates her. She's so formal about it. Rose feels a sinking in her stomach. Is this how it's going to be? Two acquaintances meeting in the grocery store? She hopes not. Eloise gives her a hug, and when she pulls away, tears fill her eyes and she says, "I hope it's a girl."

The key is to squeeze lemon on the watermelon before everything else. It's a perfect summer salad: sweet, sour, and savory. Which actually describes my life right now. Jeremy's deal, Theo's betrayal, my trip to Laguna. Just two more days and I'll be there.

The salad is a hit and sells out by eight o'clock. I'm proud, and happy for the temporary distraction. But now it's all racing back. How could Theo do that? Am I really that bad a judge of character?

When I leave, I find Bell in the alley, smoking. I know he must be beyond stressed out, because he quit five years ago.

"Dad. Don't do this."

"Sorry, Ollie. It's all a bit crazy for me right now."

I take the cigarette from his mouth and put it out.

"Is it about the house or the restaurant?" I ask.

"Both. I never pictured it coming to this."

He shakes his head and I try to cheer him up. "Well, Jeremy is getting a huge record deal now. Has he told you yet?"

Bell looks up to the sky, I think half expecting it to fall.

"Yes. And well he should. But that's his money."

"Dad, your whole life has been dedicated to us. It's our turn to start helping out."

He gives me a soulful look. Bell always taught me to accept compliments with grace, to not be afraid of being helped, that we can't do everything alone.

"Yes. You're right. Now off you go."

CHAPTER 23

The next day, Enrique wakes me up from an after-work nap.

"Ollie, I need a favor for you."

"A favor *from* me."

"Yes. There is a dinner. Tonight. The house of Len, the studio guy who loved your bruschetta. Bell will be at FOOD and can't come, obviously, but I have to go and I need you to come with me. This film he's doing, it has gotten the green light, and it's about ballet, and he's paying me to consult with him. I don't know if it will be enough to get us out of our hole, but it could be a lot. I can't show up alone. When he says bring someone, you bring someone, it doesn't matter who. But I'm sure he will be happy to see you."

Enrique is really trying, and maybe it's because I'm groggy, but it touches me.

"Okay," I say.

"Great. Six o'clock."

"Okay, Papá, okay."

He does an arabesque.

On our way to Bel Air, I secretly thank myself that I put a good dress on. Yes, it's secondhand, but the style is timeless and suits my body. Enrique is wearing a sports coat I've never seen before. And he's done his hair with a part, making him look very *Mad Men*.

When we arrive at Len's house, a giant gate is opened. The driveway goes on forever. The place looks like Versailles, or what I've seen of it in textbooks. When we get to the front door, what appear to be British butlers greet us and lead us down a long hallway adorned with paintings that are probably original van Goghs. On the way, a waiter pops out a side door and hands us each a glass of champagne.

"Just have a sip," Enrique whispers.

The house is completely overdone, with ornate gilt-framed mirrors and lush red carpets, crystal chandeliers, and intricate moldings. We finally reach a room where Len, presumably his assistant, and two other gentlemen sit. We all say hello, and Len looks surprised to see me. "Miss Bruschetta! What a pleasure!"

Enrique clears his throat and looks proud.

Len smiles and says, "Great. So, what do you think of the house?"

"Understated," I blurt out, Bell's ironic edge coming through me. Thankfully, Len thinks it's hilarious and cracks up. The other two guys look at me funny. Swarms of servants surround us with appetizers and more drinks. I see those frozen quiche things and almost gasp. But there are some fresh tuna rolls, so I let it pass. I believe that all food can be prepared in an enjoyable way, whether it's rice and beans or filet mignon, but a kajillionaire serving mini frozen quiches? Do you know how long it takes to make quiche? If you have the crust, basically about five minutes.

They talk about the film for a while, and I zone out, thinking about the Laguna trip—what I'll wear, how I'll sit, what Lola and I will discuss as I look around for Jane. When I tune back in, I manage to gather that one of the guys, Ross, is the director, and the other is the writer, but that's about all I retain. Enrique is on fire, making everyone laugh and being as charming as possible without grating on them.

"I started when I was seven. My mother took me to a ballet, and I knew right then. My classmates were mean about it, but they were just jealous because I got to hang out with beautiful girls all day. Of course, they didn't know that I was batting for the other team."

After a while, there is a general sense of bewilderment

due to the fact that dinner has not yet been served. The drinks have been refilled, but the appetizers lie in sad heaps on the trays, long discarded. Finally, a man I assume to be the head butler comes out and whispers extensively in Len's ear, making him turn bright red. Afterward, Len clears his throat and says, "I'm afraid my chef is a no-show. Would you all mind terribly if we ordered in?"

I picture us eating out of containers in this beautiful house, and it just seems wrong. "Well, I could take a look and maybe whip something up?" I offer.

Len's eyes widen, and even the writer, who has been a little stiff all night, seems to loosen at the mention of a home-cooked meal.

Next thing you know, I am amid all the black-and-white-uniformed people who apparently only know how to unwrap food and pour drinks. I open the huge pantry doors and see a large box of whole-wheat penne. I fill a big pot with water, pinch in some salt, and search the fridge for some sauce ingredients. Someone named Pepe hands me some really good olive oil, like he knows that's exactly what I was looking for. I find a block of feta cheese, a clove of garlic, some tomato paste, and a half-filled container of heavy cream. As I frantically try to put it all together, the staff watches me, their mouths open. While the pasta boils, I grab the cookbook out of my bag. Toward the end there's the recipe for beef stew and Rose's familiar writing underneath:

Made for a party.
But then scratched and made meatballs.
Sometimes you have to just stick with what you know.

I slip the book back into my bag and strain the pasta. I scour the place for the finishing touch, that last component that will make the dish. There's nothing in the pantry or in the small compartments of the fridge. Defeated, I turn around to a smile from Pepe, who leads me with his finger to a narrow door that looks like it once held an ironing board, the kind that folds out. I open it and *boom*, there it is—black truffle. I shave some on top of the dish and give the staff the go-ahead to take it out. They are all giggling with delight.

Halfway through the meal, Len raises his wineglass and says, "Bruschetta, you've done it again!"

"Just don't start calling me Penne. Bruschetta has a better ring to it," I reply.

Enrique gives me a smile so wide it looks like his face might fall off. Since his mouth is full, the director can only say "Mmmm," while the writer kisses the tips of his fingers. In that moment, all my worry is lifted and I feel like I am exactly where I need to be. I think about Theo, telling me that very same thing. He seemed so genuine. So kind. How could it all have been an act?

They talk more about ballet, and I'm amazed at how articulate Enrique is. It's strange when you see your parents in real-life situations and realize how intelligent they are.

"People are intimidated. But you don't have to know the positions to understand it. You simply have to watch it," Enrique says. "For the dancer, it is all mind-driven. If ballet were a sport, it would be tennis. Yes, the physicality is important, but a lot of it is in the head. And you have to train, train, train. It is cruel, really, for the dancer. Always striving for perfection. I was dancing in Mexico's greatest company, and I still never felt good enough. But there is nothing in this life that could take me so far away. It's like living in another world, on the stage, and when you get close, when you can almost smell the perfection, magic happens."

Silence falls over the room as people wipe up the remaining sauce on their plates with bread. When you make pasta, it is very important not to oversauce. After you are finished, there should be enough sauce left for two swipes.

As the coffee is served, the writer guy starts talking about the film they're shooting, and how the cast is unreliable. I excuse myself to go to the bathroom, but before I'm out of the room I hear Ross, who has been frantically texting someone, say that his location manager is "back off the wagon" and screwed up booking their restaurant shoot for the next day.

"So basically I need a fully working restaurant for forty-eight hours starting tomorrow at noon," he says. "Good times."

I turn around and walk back to the table, unable to

contain my excitement. Enrique's eyes light up. He has the same idea. I put my hand on the director's shoulder. At first he's shocked, but then he says, "Yes?"

"About the restaurant. We may be able to help you out with that."

CHAPTER 24

I convince Janice that being on a set would help me in my job, so she lets me leave at one o'clock.

When I get to FOOD, I barely recognize it. There are several trucks parked outside, a slew of boom microphones, and a city of lights. Production assistants swarm the place with their black shirts and walkie-talkies. I find Bell in the kitchen, telling the cooks to pretend it's just a regular night, as that's what the director wants. When he sees me his face brightens and he motions for me to come into the walk-in cooler. He sits on a box of potatoes and gets choked up, but this time out of joy.

"The onions?" I ask him.

He smiles.

"Ollie, I can't believe this. They're paying us fifteen

thousand dollars. It's not going to solve everything, but it will buy us some time."

"Great. Maybe you can form a relationship with the studio, you know?"

He smiles again, but there's a hint of condescension. "Look at you, my little businesswoman."

"Dad, we've got to save this place. It's your everything."

He wipes at his left eye with the dish towel he's holding.

"Ollie, *you're* my everything. Now let's get out of here, it's freezing."

"Okay."

When we come out of the cooler, I notice there's a crowd on the street checking out what's going on. The trailers for the talent are here, and Ross is scoping the place out. When he notices me, he runs over and gives me a hug. He takes me into the biggest trailer, where the main character, whom he calls "the star of the picture," is warming up. Her name is Jasmine, of course, and she's tiny, with short spiky red hair and big blue eyes. A mini version of me, if I chopped off my hair and starved myself. I've seen her in a commercial for something. She looks bored. A heavyset woman is dabbing powder on her cheeks.

"This is a crucial scene," Ross tells me, "and the place is perfect. Our girl here has got a secret, and she needs to reveal it in a public place."

"I'm telling my boyfriend that I'm a lesbian," Jasmine says, as if it's not a big deal.

"And . . . ," Ross says.

"And I'm in love with his sister."

The makeup woman gasps. Ross smiles and says, "I didn't write it, I'm just directing it."

Ross continues taking me around, and there are three assistants hovering like flies around him. One of them has been trying to give him a bottle of water for twenty minutes. He doesn't even seem to notice them but is fixated on me, and even though I'm not sure why, it feels good to seem important.

"What should she order?" Ross asks me. "I mean, what should she be eating? Nothing too complicated, but I want to show that she's still hungry. That she's so comfortable with her revelation, she can still have an appetite."

"How about a salad with a protein?"

"Perfect."

"Tuna or chicken?"

"Definitely chicken," he says. "Tuna is too feminine."

I smile and he says, "You see how important my job is? I constantly have to worry about things like protein. These people," he whispers, pointing to the gaggle of assistants, "probably don't even know how to make a sandwich. Their idea of lunch is a Snapple and a cigarette."

We choose the table by the window because, as Ross tells me, "Film is all about reflection."

He is called away by the arrival of the male star, and Bell comes up and whispers in my ear, "Jude Law is here!" I smile and follow him into the main dining room. Sure enough, it's Jude Law. He doesn't have an entourage, and he's joking around with one of the PAs. I've never cared about the few celebrities I've met with Enrique, but this is totally different. Kind of a rush, actually, especially because we're at FOOD.

The first time Ross yells "Action," the whole room takes on a sense of magic, a heightened expanse of time. All the preparation has led up to this moment, and everyone is wishing for the perfect take. Jude Law's reaction to the news is calm during the first take, and he starts moving the silverware around, distracting himself, I guess. Jasmine is surprisingly good, her eyes boring into him effortlessly. The news comes out fairly believable, and I'm impressed by her craft. Jude's character gets more and more angry as the scene progresses, and he ends up swiping the whole table with his hand on the last take, breaking two of our glasses.

As I walk home, I realize I still have Theo's necklace on. I've worn it pretty much all the time since he gave it to me. I wonder what he could possibly have to say, why he went to Jeremy looking for me. How could he have been so blatant? I knew there was probably someone else from before. There's no way someone as cute as Theo spent a year without hooking up with someone. I wouldn't have expected him to. But not now—not after we . . . I just wanted everything to be out in the open, but I didn't pressure him to tell me what I wanted to know because I didn't want to push him away. I feel like he walked into the agency for a reason, and it's connected to other reasons, like routes on a map. The trouble is, no one tells you which turns to take or even where you're going. And now we've reached a dead end.

Jeremy stops by Saturday morning, and as I pour us each a bowl of cereal he looks at me suspiciously.

"You're not experimenting with drugs, are you?"

I have to laugh, seeing Jeremy's face, trying to look like a concerned adult.

"Not unless Advil is all the rage."

He smiles and takes a spoonful of his cereal.

"You never make cereal. It's not a dish."

I shrug. My bag is already packed upstairs and my stomach is twisted in a hundred knots. I can't tell if I'm excited or scared about Laguna, or if the sick feeling inside me is all about Theo.

Jeremy eats with his mouth slightly open, and though it's pretty gross, I'm used to it.

"What's going on with the Dads?"

"Well, the movie shoot bought the restaurant some time, with some left over for the house, but I'm not sure how much more we need for that."

"What?"

"They owe a lot of back payments on the mortgage."

"Crap. It doesn't end. This deal better go through."

"Yeah." I sigh.

Jeremy slurps up the milk at the bottom of his bowl and looks at me. For a moment, all the confidence is drained from his face. He looks like a frightened animal waiting for someone to save him. I glance at his guitar leaning against the wall and think about his dream, how hard he's worked and how he's never given up. I hug him and whisper in his ear, "It will go through."

"Hope so. Thanks for the Honey Bunches of Oats."

"They don't call me Chef for nothing."

He grabs his guitar and does a little hop toward the door.

CHAPTER 25

On the way to Laguna, Lola tells me that she actually asked Jin out.

"That's awesome!"

"I think he was a bit flustered—don't you think that's a good sign?"

"Yes."

She asks me why I don't have the necklace on, and I decide that I can tell her about what I saw without completely breaking down, so I do. She's just as baffled as I am.

"Well, we've got other food on our plate at the moment, don't we?"

She enters the HOV lane, and I tell her about Jeremy putting an old scarecrow in the passenger seat of Bell's car just so he could ride the lane to his friend's concert in

Long Beach. She laughs. The road stretches out before us like a chance.

"When I said goodbye to Bell, I could feel the secret in the air between us," I say. "It's the one part of this whole thing that feels off. Bell thinks I'm just going to hang out with you. Which is not a lie, but also not the total truth."

I think of Rose not telling Kurt the whole Eloise story.

"Well, if it's bugging you, why don't you call him right now and tell him?"

"I feel like that would be a cop-out. I'll just tell him in person when I get back. He lied to me about my mother remaining nameless, so in a way we're even."

"I've told you this before, but I like the way you think, Livie."

Our hotel is perched on a cliff on the coastline, and as Lola checks us in I sit on one of the white couches and stare out the window. There really is nothing more beautiful than the ocean. For the second time since the Stingray Trauma, I don't get a panicked feeling. It actually looks approachable.

A father and his young son step up to the glass, and I hear the boy say, "All the oceans in the world are connected."

The father looks at him, and I can tell he's amazed that the kid has grasped this concept. As they walk away I think about what he said about the ocean. Maybe my fear comes from more than the stingray. Maybe I've always just been overwhelmed by the power of it.

I guess I look exhausted, because when Lola comes back, she asks what's wrong.

"I'm just tired."

"How does a nap sound?"

"Great."

"Okay, I'm going to have a late lunch with my cousin, so let's meet in the lobby at seven."

"Sounds good."

Our room is huge and smells like fresh lemon. I lie on the bed closest to the window and listen to the long, slow breath of the sea. Despite everything, the sound of the waves has always been soothing to me. I think of the surfer girl whose arm was bitten off by a shark, and how two months later she was back in the water. Having that kind of courage is unfathomable to me. But here I am in Laguna, in search of my mother.

I sleep for a good hour or so, and when I wake up I decide to walk down to the cute part of town where the galleries, cafes, and clothing stores are. I walk into a shop called Surf and Sport, and right in front is a mannequin wearing a yellow bikini with a white rose on the bottom part. A girl about my age walks up and says, "Pretty, right? We just got those in."

"I know someone named Rose," I tell her. "Maybe I should get it."

"You'd look super cute in it," the girl says.

It's thirty-nine dollars, and I only have thirty-five. The girl looks over her shoulder to see if her manager's around, then says, "It's cool. No worries."

"Thanks," I tell her, and she smiles at me like we're best friends.

When I get back to the hotel, I put on the suit and it fits perfectly. I wrap a towel around myself and slip into my flip-flops. I take the stairs down to the beach, and the sand is warm from a full day of being sun-kissed. The waves are tame, and the water is very clear, its color hovering right between blue and green.

As I walk closer to the edge, I touch the rose on my suit, thinking of her and the courageous surfer girl. Why can't I be just as brave? When the first wave runs over my feet I laugh a little. I'm not sure what's funny about it, but everything feels like it's in slow motion, like I'm watching myself go in farther and farther until the water is almost at my waist. The line of the fading sun makes a million sparks on the top of the water, and they're all pointing directly at me.

CHAPTER 26

In the end, I don't go under and really swim, but it's a start. When I get back to the hotel, I shower and put on my polka-dot dress (a hand-me-down from Lola). Then I sit on the floor in front of the mirror and wonder if all this is really happening. I just stepped into the ocean, and my mother is within three hundred yards of me right now.

The message light on the room phone is blinking red. I check it and it's Theo. He sounds very upset and must have been on his cell in a bad area because I can barely make out what he's saying. Another reason I can't stand cell phones.

I walk to the window, wondering what dumb excuse he came up with. I think about calling him back, but I'm here on a mission and I can't let a boy crowd my thoughts.

Instead of calling Theo, I decide to check in with Bell, as promised. He sounds happy that I've called. I tell him about the hotel, and he tells me that it looks like Jeremy actually didn't get the record deal, but he got a development deal.

"What does that mean?" I ask.

"Well, they're still giving him an advance, but they want to take six months to develop his sound."

"Oh."

"It's still good news, and there's a good chance it will lead to a record deal."

I don't tell Bell that I'm about to see my mother, but I do tell him I went into the ocean. I can almost see him beaming through the phone.

"Thattagirl!"

"Well, I didn't actually swim, but I went in above my knees."

"Well, baby steps, as they say. Just be careful out there, you know, in the world."

I smile. "I can look after myself, Dad."

After I hang up, I lie on the plush bed and stare at the ceiling, thinking about everything that has led me to this day, this moment. I take ten deep breaths, like my seventh-grade drama teacher taught me, pretending there's a small balloon I'm inflating in my stomach. It's a relaxation technique. I tell myself: *This is where I'm meant to be. I went into the ocean, and tonight, I will meet my mother.*

I flip through the cookbook again to see if I missed any

of Rose's notes. I've read all the ones in the margins. But on one of the blank pages at the back of the book, there's a poem without a date.

> The day you left, you told me
> There is nothing as sweet
> As the sound of my laugh.
> Well, I have made the bread
> And I have stood in the rain
> To hide the tears.
>
> We are soldiers of a similar war
> And we fight to understand
> What the fight is for.
>
> I hope one day I will laugh
> And wherever you are, you will hear it.

I lie back on the pillows, pressing the book against my loudly beating heart.

Lola bursts into the room and says, "You look smashing! I'm ready, I swear, just give me a minute."

"How was your cousin?"

"Oh, he's a bit geeky, but it was fun. I didn't tell him about Mum. She doesn't want anyone to know. You know how we Brits are with messy, emotional things."

"Maybe she's just hopeful."

"Perhaps. But now, my friend, it's time to meet *your* mother."

As we head down to the lobby, I wonder if I will always think of the psychic when I'm in an elevator. She was right—this summer has been "pivotal," to say the least. When she mentioned the "choices," maybe she was referring to deciding whether to find my mother. Part of me hopes my mother will be happy to see me and we'll form some sort of bond. She *is* a cook, after all. Maybe we can trade recipes, and she can be there if I ever have my own child. I realize I've gotten carried away and take a breath to slow myself down. We reach the lobby and head outside into the circular courtyard, stopping at the large fountain.

"So this is it, huh?"

"Yes. But remember, Livie, you don't want to rush into it."

"So basically I should run in there and scream 'Mommy!' at the top of my lungs?"

She laughs and says, "Maybe try a different approach."

I'm not sure if it's the cobblestone sidewalk, but as the orange awning comes into view again, I feel unsteady on my legs. I grab Lola's arm for extra support and take ten more really deep breaths. Again I imagine the balloon in my stomach, gently filling all the way up with air.

"Let's just be normal," Lola says.

"Right."

"Look at it this way. You have the upper hand. You can tell her, or not. Your choice."

She's right. I really should try to unfreak myself out.

We're greeted by a young waiter who seats us by tilting his head toward a table at the front. I glance out the window before we sit down. The sun has sunk through the trees, and there's a yellow, almost full moon starting to rise.

A woman comes to greet us. She's wearing a thin sweater and jeans, and is using a cane to help her walk. When she turns to face me, I hold my breath. She looks, and I'm not kidding, like Julie Andrews. Her hair is the exact color of mine and her eyes are the same shape. The sensation is like looking into a mirror of the future, and I have to look away.

I nod, finally let out my breath, and blink away the beginning of a tear. She smiles and hands us the menus. Her fingers are long and delicate, and adorned with only one simple silver ring. There are some burn marks on her forearms, which tells me she not only runs the place, she's also doing a fair amount of the cooking.

"Hi. I'm Olivia," I say. Lola gives me a look. I have no idea why I just introduced myself.

She looks at me curiously, as if she's almost recognizing something, but then snaps back into hostess mode.

"Hi, Olivia, I'm Jane. What brings you to Laguna?"

I am so not prepared for this question.

"I'm visiting my cousin," Lola says, "and Olivia's never been here, so here we are! And we heard this is the best place, so we had to come—Livie here is quite the cook herself."

206

"Wonderful. Perhaps I'll give you a tour of our high-tech kitchen a little later. But for now, let's get you a drink."

"Fizzy water, please," Lola says, "and she'll have orange juice. It's all she drinks."

I think Lola is starting to get more excited than I am.

"Coming right up," Jane says, and smiles right at me. I feel like jumping into her arms.

"Oh my Lord, she looks just like you!" Lola stage-whispers when Jane is out of sight. "It's like a movie."

The waiter brings us some bread and olive tapenade, and even though I'm literally shaking and can't fathom eating anything, I am curious to try it. There's something different about it, and I think I know what it is. It's one of the best tapenades I've ever tasted.

"What?" Lola asks.

"Sun-dried tomato," I reply. "The marinated kind. That's the signature touch. Just pure olive is too salty, too boring. The SDT gives it some balance."

"SDT? That's dangerously close to STD."

I almost choke on my water. I'm trying to act normal, but I don't think it's working.

"I feel like she kind of recognized me. This is so surreal."

"Just keep breathing. She seems very chill."

My mother comes back with the sparkling water and my juice. I try not to stare, but it's impossible not to. The woman gave birth to me, and I haven't seen her in almost seventeen years.

I try to imagine what I look like to her. Is the polka-dot dress too much? I start getting paranoid that I must seem like a nervous wreck, but Jane's gaze warms me like a blanket, so I am briefly calmed.

"Olivia says there's SDT in your tapenade," Lola says.

"Good tongue," Jane says, impressed.

"Thanks," I reply, half under my breath. I take a sip of my orange juice and try to set it back down, but completely miss the table. The glass crashes on the floor and juice goes everywhere. Jane motions for the busboy like this sort of thing happens all the time. In a frantic haze, I apologize and excuse myself to go to the bathroom, and when I look in the mirror I see that I'm bright red. I splash my face with cold water and tell myself to suck it up. Yes, it's my mother. But I don't want to give myself away until I'm ready. I want this on my terms.

As I come out, I notice Jane expediting some of the orders, turning on her heel and using the cane as sort of a kick start.

"Oh my God, I'm such a spaz," I tell Lola as I sit down.

"Livie, no one's bothered. Just breathe. They poured you more juice. But maybe keep the glass near the center of the table this time."

"Good idea."

For the rest of our meal, my mother doesn't return, and I'm thankful actually. I keep stealing glances toward the kitchen. I can see some large pots that look like something Julia Child would have used. So clearly she was being sarcastic when she said high-tech. Occasionally I can see the top of Jane's head below the small expediting station. The place has filled up, and it looks like she's working hard. I think there are only two other prep cooks. As Lola goes on about something Jin-related, I get more of an appetite, and after the first bite of my roast chicken I realize I'm starving. Sometimes it just takes a taste of something to get your hunger going. Like when Theo first kissed me, all I could think about was lying next to him, feeling his whole body touch mine. The first kiss was just the beginning. But was our last kiss the end?

This chicken is one of the best I've ever had. Jane must know the trick of putting some butter under the skin.

"So, Livie," Lola whispers, "what do you think?"

I don't say anything, and Lola looks at me expectantly.

"Of the chicken?"

"No, of your mother!" Lola says a little too loudly.

"I don't know what to think. I'm just trying not to pass out. It's weird. I mean, if she gave me up when I was two days old, why would she want to see me now?"

Lola looks toward the kitchen and smiles a little. "I'm not sure she will. But that was a long time ago. Why don't you come back tomorrow if you don't feel ready now? Didn't your boss say she lives upstairs?"

I look up, trying to imagine her place, if she decorated it like I would, if she's neat. In our house, mine is the only room that's always tidy. I definitely didn't get that from Bell or Enrique. And Jeremy, well, he's a total slob.

"I could see myself having her kind of life."

We finally get up to leave, and as we step outside, dark clouds are quickly covering the stars. The air is thicker, and a strong wind rattles the poplars, their petals floating everywhere. In the short time we were inside, the weather completely flipped.

The wind is so loud we barely talk on the way back to the hotel. In the elevator, the bellman notices our wind-blown hair and says, "Crazy, huh?" We nod and smile, and he says, "I hear L.A. is getting hit even harder."

We settle into our room, and I distract myself with some bad but somehow entertaining reality TV while Lola takes a bath. Eventually I find a cooking show and become transfixed. As I get sleepy, I flip through once more, and on CNN there's breaking news on the storm in Los Angeles. There's a reporter getting whipped by the wind, and it looks like the rain is actually going sideways. She's saying it's the worst storm L.A. has seen in over a decade, and they show clips of Sunset Boulevard, right by my house. My eyes bulge and my stomach tightens at the sight of three palm trees on my street—the one constant in my life—broken and splayed on the boulevard, their leaves already being run over by cars.

My palm trees. Those towering, skinny monsters with mop heads looking over everything. I never thought they would come down, not in a million years. My face is still frozen, and I'm staring at the footage but not really hearing the words the reporter is saying. I take out the cookbook and write a note to Rose:

The palm trees have fallen. I feel like a part of me broke with them. Is that how you felt with Matthew? Rose, you did the right thing, going back to Kurt. Maybe Eloise will find someone, and she'll move on and you can go back to being best friends. Or not. Either way, you lived as you knew how, and sometimes that's all we can do.

CHAPTER 27

I get up very early and again have to tell myself that what is happening to me is real, that I'm not dreaming. I met my mother last night, and the palm trees have fallen. Will I miss Theo forever? Does Rose still miss Matthew? Is nothing in life constant? I think about Bell, Enrique, Jeremy, and Lola. They have been constant. But in the end, it's just me. We are only here temporarily, so we have to make it last. Speak the truth, follow our hearts, and break the rules once in a while.

Lola is a morning person and is already awake when I sit up. She comes out of the bathroom wearing a hotel robe, putting moisturizer on her face.

"This is the day," I tell her. "I'm going to meet her for real."

"Bravo, Livie. You want me to come?"

I look into the mirror and try to see Jane looking back. I will myself to have the courage that Rose had.

"No, thanks."

"You fine walking there?"

"Yes, it's only like a mile, if that."

Lola sprays her hair with some product that makes it shine and says, "Okay, Livie, then I'm off for some shopping. It's going to be fine, either way. If she's nice, then great, but if not, at least you found out. And let us not forget that you have two awesome dads. Nothing is going to change that."

"You're right."

"Call my cell when you're back at the hotel and I'll come meet you. Good luck, dear. I'll be rooting for you while I try on sundresses."

After Lola leaves, I call Bell again. He sounds a little down.

"The storm has been like an apocalypse. So much damage. Luckily the restaurant is okay. What about down there?"

"Just wind last night. I can't believe the palm trees are gone."

"You've always loved them, even when you were a toddler."

"I know. Anyway, what's the latest?"

"Well, Ross has booked the restaurant for filming again. Another movie."

"Yay! So that will buy you more time then?"

"More than that. I think this could change everything."
I hear him sigh. "I think we're going to be okay. So, how's
your trip going?"

"Great."

Before I blurt out anything about my mother, I change
the subject and ask about Jeremy.

"He's doing really well. There's been more talk about a
manager."

"I can't believe it."

"I know. Well, I miss you, Ollie. It's so weird that you're
becoming an adult. I'm not ready to let you go."

"I'm still Ollie, Dad. I always will be," I tell him. But I'm
not sure it's the whole truth.

I peek in the window of Jane Armont's restaurant, and
it's completely empty. I walk slowly up the stairs to the
right of the main entrance, which lead to a small porch.
I stand there for a while telling myself to just do it, re-
membering what Lola said, trying to summon the bravery
in Rose's heart. Despite my finding a way to focus more
on myself this summer, I still believe that we are a patchwork of the people around us—the ones we choose to
learn from.

This is the moment. I raise my hand and knock twice. At
first I don't hear anything, but then a voice says something

I can't make out, and the door opens just a crack. When she sees me, she opens it up all the way.

"Hi, Jane."

"Hello there. . . . Can I help you with something?"

Where do I start? I can feel my right leg shake a little.

"Yes. Could I . . . could I talk to you about something?"

"Well, I suppose so. Would you like to come in?"

"That would be great."

Her living room is quaint and cozy, and there are fresh-cut flowers in a large vase on the table. I was right—I got the neat gene from her. She offers me a seat. She doesn't have the cane but still walks funny. It takes all the strength I have to quell the trembling inside me as I look her in the eye. She is beautiful.

"You used to live in L.A., right?"

"Years and years ago, yes. How do you know that?"

I will myself to just say it.

"And you gave a child up for adoption?"

The bomb has dropped. The words linger in the air. Her hand goes to her mouth, her eyes widen, and her face pales. For a second she looks like an ice sculpture.

"It's me."

I swear she stops breathing. Then she clears her throat and says, "Would you excuse me for a minute?"

"Sure."

She goes into the bathroom for what seems like a lifetime. Is she going to come out and tell me to leave?

When she finally returns, she looks visibly shaken, as if her body is crumbling in on itself. Her lower lip quivers, and a teardrop slips from her left eye and lands on her gray T-shirt, making a small blotch. Then she walks over to me and places her hands on my shoulders and all I can think is *My mother is touching me.*

"Come, come."

She leads me through her bright kitchen and out the back door, down the stairs that lead to a small garden.

"I'm going to need a drink. How old . . ."

"Almost seventeen."

She's doing the math in her head.

"Yes, of course. How did you find . . ."

"I saw your name on the birth certificate. I Googled you and not much came up, but as it turned out, my boss knew you. Janice Tucker, the casting director . . ."

"Well . . . I honestly don't know what to say."

I see what looks like anger in her face, then confusion, then a strange peace as she says, "When I saw you last night, I felt something." She puts her arms around herself and leans her head back. Then she stands up and says, "I'll be right back. I want to hear your story, and I want to tell you mine. I just have to get someone to take a meeting for me. Wine sellers."

I start to protest and she says, "No. Sit. This is . . . well, extraordinary."

She has a little trouble getting up the stairs, and I wonder once again what the cane is for. I guess it will all come out soon. I'm left in her garden, stunned, tears drying on my face. I think she may be right. Today is extraordinary.

CHAPTER 28

Jane Armont, the woman who carried me inside her for nine months and gave birth to me, is wearing a black sweater and a tangerine-colored scarf. We walk slowly along the beach near her restaurant, looking out at the sprawl of the Pacific, with its frothy edges and scattered whitecaps flashing in irregular patterns.

"I went in, yesterday," I say. "Sort of."

"Ah. Isn't it great?"

"Well, yes. Only I just realized that yesterday."

"How so?"

"Since I was really young I've been afraid of the ocean. I stepped on a stingray."

Jane pauses and gently massages the brass dome at the top of her cane. "Those stingrays will do it to you every time."

I smile. I feel comfortable and awkward at the same time. It's kind of like a blind date with someone you feel like you already know. "Well, I think I may be over it."

"Good for you." We look at each other, and she can sense what I'm about to ask, so she just starts talking.

"Why don't I go first? Your birth father was in the navy. He was stationed in Orange County and we met at a museum opening. I was looking at a painting of an old man at sea. He came up behind me and said, 'You complete the picture.' I remember at the time thinking it was a silly pickup line, but when I looked at his face, he wasn't wearing a mask. He was just being himself. On our first date he took me to meet his mother."

"Wow." I kick off my flip-flops and we sit on a large piece of driftwood.

"His mother was a potter, and kind of a hippie. Over the next few weeks, we went bowling, watched trains, did all these things I never expected to be doing with him. You see, he looked really mainstream, yet he was anything but. It's a lesson, really."

I nod, already knowing that.

"So about three weeks after we met, well, you happened. We had used protection, but . . ."

I remember that in sex ed they told us condoms are 98 percent effective.

"Two percent," I say.

She sips her iced tea, swallows, and says, "Exactly."

"Then what happened?"

"He got transferred to Delaware. I found out that I was

pregnant too late for an abortion. Well, not exactly too late, but I didn't want to risk complications. So I carried you . . ." She dabs at her forehead with the small handkerchief she's holding. "I carried you to term, as they say."

I feel my face get hot. "So I was supposed to be aborted?"

"Well, you do believe in a woman's choice, right?"

"Of course, but didn't you even consider keeping me?"

She gathers her hair to the left side of her head with her elegant fingers. "No. I was way too young. I was only twenty-one. I'm sorry if that sounds callous. But I needed to live, you know? I had dreams, and they did not involve diapers and day care. It was hard, maybe even the hardest thing I've done, because I got used to you being inside me. For the first few years I felt a lot of guilt, but then I had faith that you were in a better place, with parents who wanted to be parents. But I never stopped wondering. There's an older man who washes my floors at the restaurant. He was the only person I told. I figured it was safe to tell someone like him, a person who wasn't very visible in my life. You know what's strange? Recently, this woman came into the restaurant, a psychic. She loved the food and told me she would read me for free. She actually told me that someday you would walk through the door."

My jaw drops.

"That is so weird. I wonder if it was the same woman who read *me*. Did she have a streak of gray in her hair?"

"I don't remember."

My mother looks at me in a way that would normally embarrass me, but I don't feel myself blushing.

Three towheaded kids plop down right next to us and start throwing sand at one another. The mother catches up with them and says, "Stop it," but they pretend not to hear.

"This may sound odd," I say, "but I just wanted to know that a piece of me was out there, living and breathing. In the beginning I never cared. But after school got out this year everything changed—I mean, *everything*. I started to really feel your absence. And I felt like there was more and more possibility in the world. I became more curious as each day passed."

"So you haven't always been this proactive?"

I look past her at the large expanse of sea. "Not exactly. I was pretty shy growing up."

"I find that hard to believe."

"It's true. One more question, though. Did you ever tell him?"

My mother looks down at her hands, takes a deep breath. "Olivia, this is one of my biggest regrets in life. I traveled to Delaware to do just that, and it all backfired. There was another woman living with him; she was caustic. And he wasn't the same. I was too proud, or selfish, or whatever you want to call it, so I never told him."

"So where is he now?"

"I haven't been in contact with him since that day, about five months before you were born."

At this moment, I can't even think about who my father

is. I already have two of those. I don't have room in my head for another one.

"But I want to hear about *you*," she says, adjusting her scarf. "I want to hear about your parents. What's your mother like?"

A memory of Enrique picking me up from school on his Vespa flashes in my mind. "I have two dads."

"Oh. Do they know you're here?"

"No. I mean, they know I'm in Laguna, but not the whole story."

"I want the whole story," she says, her eyes warm and disarming.

I just start talking, and the more I do, the more normal I feel. I tell her all about Silver Lake, about Jeremy and Bell and Enrique, and about my specials at FOOD. Then I recount the day I met the psychic in the elevator, and Hank leading me to Rose's book (which I show her), the safe-deposit box, reuniting with Theo only to have him betray me, the journey that brought me here. I remember teachers always telling me that I'm a good listener, and I realize I must have gotten that from my mother, who seems to take in deeply everything I'm saying. Then I tell her about my dream of studying at Le Cordon Bleu, and I see a flash of light in her eyes, her mouth forming an oval shape.

"What?" I ask.

"Nothing, that's wonderful."

A family of four passes us by and smiles at us. Maybe they can sense the heavy reunion vibes in the air.

"I tell you what. Why don't you come by the restaurant tomorrow? We'll cook something together. Would you like that?"

This time I look at her as if *she* dropped from the sky.

"Yes, I would."

"Great. I have . . . an appointment in the morning, so I'll meet you there at noon?"

"Sounds great."

For the next few moments, before we part ways, we just smile at each other, and I feel light-headed but strangely calm.

I lie on the hotel bed, thoughts and questions buzzing around my brain like trapped insects. *Will my dads be mad? Why did her face fall when she mentioned her appointment? Does that have to do with the cane? What are we going to cook?*

I phone Janice to ask if I can have Monday off. She sounds annoyed until I tell her I'm in Laguna. Then I call Lola and tell her about the plan to cook with my mother, and ask if we can leave tomorrow instead of today. She's thrilled and says, "Of course!"

The phone rings, and it's Jeremy. "How's the Orange Curtain?"

"Great, but I never got to tell you congrats!"

"It's not a deal yet, but thanks, sis."

"Well, when you're a big star, I can be your personal chef."

"Gazpacho every day!"

I hear him shut a door; then he says softly, "Ol, with the money from the movie companies, the Dads had enough to deal with the restaurant and some of the back mortgage for the house, but not all of it. I guess things haven't been great for a while. But I took half of my advance on the development deal and paid the rest of the mortgage payments for the last few months plus the next two, so everything should be cool now."

"Jeremy, that's unbelievable." After all the times our dads and I have helped Jeremy out of his messes, it's so nice to hear this. Maybe he has really grown up. I can feel my eyes sting with emotion. "That's the best news I've heard in a long time, besides . . ."

"Besides what?"

"Well, I can't get into it now. But we'll catch up when I get back. I should go. Lola's still out, but she'll be back any minute."

Jeremy takes a deep breath and sighs.

"Okay, don't do anything I wouldn't do."

I hang up and lie back, thinking that actually leaves me a lot of options.

CHAPTER 29

I show up at the restaurant exactly at noon, and though she smiles and hugs me, I can tell Jane's a little tired.

We sit down at one of the empty tables while the older man mops the floor around us. When he weaves by, he pats me on the shoulder and gives my mother a knowing look. She puts her elbows on the table and her chin in her hands.

"I know the consensus is that French is the be-all and end-all of cooking, but let me tell you a secret. The best food to cook is Italian." She flashes me a girlish grin and more color comes back into her face. "So today, you and I are going to make artichoke lasagna."

"Sounds great."

The next hour unfolds like a dream. We work together

almost seamlessly, as if we have done this a million times before. Even though I don't really know my way around her kitchen and don't want to cramp her style, the blind date feelings have diminished considerably.

After we steam the artichokes and they're cooling, I notice my mother grab her leg and wince.

"Are you okay?"

She looks at me with a blank expression, and then says, "There's something you should know. I don't know if Janice mentioned it to you."

"No."

"No, she wouldn't have. I have MS. Do you know what that is?"

Boom. Two letters that make my heartbeat skip. "Kind of."

"Have for years. It's a neurological thing, and my case, well, it's not a big deal, or at least I tell myself that."

I want to scream "No!" but instead I say, "Does it get worse?"

"Should, but maybe not. There's no way of knowing."

As we start rolling the dough I realize that this was all too good to be true. That this not-so-little glitch was as destined to occur as everything else. I suddenly feel unbearable amounts of gratitude for even being in the same room with her right now, mixed with a tinge of anger, knowing it may not last.

As we lay all the ingredients in the pans, she asks me what it was like growing up with two dads.

"Well, you learn pretty early on how ignorant some people are. I remember the day I kind of figured out that we weren't a normal family, and I got really mad at my dads. I had gotten teased by some girls at school. But L.A. is pretty liberal. I mean, I had a lesbian teacher, and another classmate of mine had two moms. I'm just lucky I didn't grow up in Kansas or something. But to me, the expression of love between two people of the same sex has always been just as natural as with a guy and a girl."

"If only everyone could have that attitude. I suppose what Bell and . . ."

"Enrique."

". . . Enrique were doing was changing the world in their own little way. I've always wondered where you ended up, but I have to say I never thought with two dads. How nice to contribute in an indirect way to the life of a non-traditional family," she muses.

We put the lasagna in the oven and start to clean up.

"You know, I wasn't much of a cook when I was your age," Jane says. "But after I had you, I wanted to get away, so I traveled all over the world. I didn't have much money, so I would stop and work until I could move again. Always in restaurants. And everywhere I went I was interested in the food, until finally in Thailand I worked as a cook. The first thing I learned to make was lemongrass soup."

"Cool. So how did you end up here?"

"Well, I spent a few years in New York and dated a man who was a food critic. I met a lot of chefs during that time.

One of them introduced me to Andre, a hotelier based out of Montreal. He's the one who owns the hotel you guys are staying in. We connected on a lot of levels, but never romantically. We built this place together, and we have a relationship—I cater some of his meetings, and his concierge sends a built-in crowd so I never have an empty seat. It works out well. You will notice, if you haven't already, that the good fortune that comes your way in life is always related to who you know. It's important to operate in an open way, and never close yourself off to possible connections. Light shines from unexpected places."

I think about Janice knowing Jane, and Enrique finding me the job. What if I had never opened that door? I wouldn't be standing here. The psychic was right—all our decisions are connected.

I notice a framed picture of a younger Jane, walking on what looks like a Montreal sidewalk with a dark man in a suit. "Have you ever been married?"

"No. Came close once, but I don't think I'm the marrying type. I'm married to this place!"

"Do you have other family?"

"Just a sister. We sort of go in and out of each other's lives. I feel that families are like braids. You drift apart but always come back together."

All of a sudden, her face lights up.

"You know, I was thinking. Maybe I could write you a reference for Le Cordon Bleu."

I'm starting to understand that somehow I have become

a person to whom good things happen. Not that I've had a lot of bad things happen to me in the past, but there's been nothing amazing, either. "I don't know what to say. Like I told you, it would be a dream to study at CB."

"Wow, you've already got the lingo. You know what? I have a slide show from all my travels. Would you like to watch it sometime?"

"I would love to."

"Great. Now, what are you going to do about your dads?"

"Well, I guess when I go home and they ask me about my trip, I'll say, 'It was great. I cooked a meal in my mother's restaurant.' They'll laugh, then get uncomfortable, and I'll begin to explain it all. Although I'm not sure everything can be explained."

We pull the lasagna out of the oven, and the cheese is perfectly browned, our homemade red sauce bubbling over the edges.

"The secret ingredient," I say.

"What?"

I tell her about the chef I met when I was a kid. The cook's handprint on the dish. "Maybe we're that for each other," I say hopefully.

She smiles and says, "Maybe so."

CHAPTER 30

While Lola paints her toenails, I fill her in on everything. My birth, the lasagna, the MS.

"Wow."

"You don't even know. But I knew there would be some kind of catch. I mean, it's already perfect that she's a chef who lives less than two hours from me. But it kills me— like, why does she have to be . . . afflicted? It makes me want to throw something."

Lola laughs, and then looks at me very seriously. "How bad is her MS?"

"I don't know. She was vague about it."

"Well, the important thing is to make the best of now. Lord knows I'm learning that with Mum. We've played a million card games since she told me."

As I watch the waves crashing in the distance outside our window, I notice a flock of birds following the lazy arm of the coastline. Thinking about my mother's MS suddenly makes everything with Theo seem less important, not so end-of-the-world. I know that, no matter what, I will survive this.

After a while, we start to pack. When I'm finished with everything else, I pick up the cookbook to put it in my bag. For the first time I notice a little gap in the pages, as if they're warped, and open it there. I see a tiny old black-and-white picture taped to the bottom of the page, and my jaw falls open in awe.

It's Rose and Kurt! They're dancing, with one arm around each other and their free arms held up, their hands clasped. I turn the picture over and see the date and an address written on it. I grab Lola's phone and look up the address. It still exists, and is less than an hour away from the hotel, in the opposite direction from home.

"Lola," I whisper. "Can I ask you one last favor?"

"Of course. What is it? What's wrong?"

"There's somewhere else I need to go. Do you think we could drive to San Juan Capistrano before we head home?" I show her the picture of Rose and Kurt, the address on the back. "I want to see if she still lives there."

"It's so close! I can't believe it. It's like . . . fate. Yes, let's.

We can leave whenever, as I already booked the room for another night so we could leave after checkout today. It's a beautiful drive too."

She's right. The road bends in slight curves, dipping and rising over the arid hills, exposing crescents of white sand and scattered sailboats on the azure ocean. The air is clean after the storm, and the world has a shine to it. Improbable as it is, I feel like everything's going to work out.

About forty-five minutes later we arrive at the address, a weathered green house on the little strand off the beach. Lola parks and says, "I'll leave you to it. I'm just going to take a wee bit of a walk."

I step up to the door and don't even think before knocking. I'm holding the picture in my hand. This is where Rose lived. A kid answers, around my age, maybe a bit older. He's wearing a Rip Curl sweatshirt and jeans, and his hair is bleached blond from the sun. I can tell immediately that he's a surfer. He smiles and seems pleasantly surprised to see me. His teeth are perfectly aligned, and his lips are plump. He looks like he could model for a surf magazine. Maybe he has.

"What's up?" he asks.

"Sorry to bother you. I was just wondering—does someone named Rose Lane live here?"

He looks confused, but then smiles again. "She was my grandmother. Why do you ask?"

Oh my God, she *did* have another child. I pull the cookbook out of my bag and show him the name on the inside cover.

He flips through it, stopping at some of the notes. "This is a trip."

I just nod, a little humbled by how ridiculously hot he is without even trying.

"Hey, do you want to come in?"

I look out and see Lola on the beach in the distance. "Sure, for a few minutes. My friend is taking a walk. I'm Olivia, by the way."

"Cool."

Surfer Boy puts some Oreo cookies on a plate and serves us lemonade. As I'm telling him the story, I feel like he might think I'm crazy. But he seems more interested the more I explain.

"So I just kind of made up my own story from the little bits and pieces in the book. And I guess I'm here to find out what really happened."

"Well, I know that Grandma Rose and Grandpa Kurt had my mom late in life, and that she was their only child. Where did you get the cookbook again?"

"L.A."

"Yeah, she lived there for a while, I know that. But I don't really remember much else about her. I was, like, seven when she died. You know, my mom should be home any minute. She'd be cool with talking to you."

Surfer Boy has this intelligent way of enunciating his words that belies his surfer image. Does he really not know how cute he is?

"Really? That would be great."

He tells me about this surfing championship he wants

to win, how he came in third last year. When he starts in on sponsorships, I'm lost in his eyes, pools of grayish blue.

A few minutes later, in walks his mother. She's tan, wearing a flowing sundress, and has chopsticks in her hair. A hip surfer mom who could either send us to bed or give us some beers, depending on her mood.

"I leave you alone for half an hour and you're entertaining pretty young ladies?" she says to him. I can tell they have more of a friend-type relationship, like me and Bell.

Surfer Boy blushes, and it's ridiculously adorable. "Olivia has a cookbook that belonged to Grandma," he says, and takes it off the table and hands it to her.

"Hi, Olivia, I'm Eloise," she says, reaching out her hand. "But people call me Ellie."

I can't blink. I am frozen. Her hand stays in the air. I try desperately to act normal and form words.

"You were named after . . ."

"My mother's friend Eloise Lautner, why?"

I give her the book and she starts flipping through the pages. "What did she do? Write her life story in here?"

"Not really," I say. "But I kind of made some assumptions."

We all take a cookie.

"I guess I just got curious about a few things," I say.

Eloise pours herself some lemonade and says, "Well, I'll help if I can."

I think of all the questions I have, but don't want to

overdo it, so I start with a simple one. "Did Eloise also have a husband at war?"

"Yes. But he never made it back."

"Is she alive?"

"Yes. She's been with the same woman for twenty-five years. They live in Topanga Canyon."

Surfer Boy is baffled that I know more about his family than he does. I was right. Eloise was a lesbian.

"And your mother and Eloise, did they reconcile?"

She gives me a funny look. "I'm not following," she says.

How do I get into it? I'm losing the line between what I fabricated and what is turning out to be real.

"Well, there's some notes in there that refer to them that made me think they had a . . . falling-out. I think it had to do with the miscarriage?"

Now Surfer Boy is wigging out. "What?"

Eloise looks at her son and says, "Your grandmother lost a child before me. I've told you." Then she turns back to me. "My mother was upset about that, as any parent would be, but their 'falling-out,' as you say, was due to something else. And I never quite knew what that was."

I do, I think. *But there's no way I'm saying anything.*

"When she was dying, a few years after my father passed, Eloise was there. She was the person who actually watched her die."

I can barely contain the emotion that is spreading over my face. Surfer Boy looks down at his shoes. I think of the line in that Death Cab for Cutie song: "Love is watching someone die."

"What is it, sweetheart?" Ellie says.

"Nothing, it's just, I guess we all need someone there when we go," I say.

"Hmm," Surfer Boy says, "this is getting sort of gloomy."

I smile and stand up. "Listen, I'm so sorry to have just showed up here, but I got attached to your family through the book, and I was so curious. And it doesn't surprise me, but you two are super nice."

Ellie gives me a hug and looks me right in the eye. "We try," she says.

"Ellie, if I left that here," I say, pointing to the cookbook, "do you think you could give it to Eloise?"

"You know what? Maybe I can arrange for you to do that yourself. Would that be better?"

"I guess so," I say.

"Well, I've got to go wash up. So nice meeting you," she says.

"You don't even know," I say, smiling like a dork.

Ellie leaves the kitchen, and Surfer Boy writes down his phone number on a notepad that's shaped like a surfboard, so that I can contact him in the future. Then he writes his name in block letters:

BLAKE.

"Well, I should go, but if it's not too stalkery, I will totally call."

"It can't really get any more stalkery," he says through a

smile. "But seriously, please do. Maybe we can hang out."
He leans forward a little, and I feel like he's going to kiss
me. I back up slightly, only because if I get closer I might
kiss him back.

"Sounds good."

He reaches past me to open the door. The wispy blond
hairs on his tanned forearm brush lightly against my
cheek. I thank him again and try my best not to trip going
down his porch stairs.

When I get to the car, Lola is already inside, sending a
text to someone. She stops and looks at me with question-
ing eyes.

"She's not alive, but I met her grandson and her daughter," I tell her.

"Really?"

We pull out of the parking spot and I open the window
a little.

"Yes."

"So, was he cute or what?"

"Beyond. The crazy thing is, you know the whole life I
created for these people? It's basically accurate."

"I guess, knowing you, that shouldn't surprise me. Did
you get his digits?"

"You know it."

"Ahhh!" Lola screeches excitedly, slapping her hands on
the steering wheel.

The rest of the way back to the hotel, I close my eyes
and let the sea breeze blow on my face, and think about

all the things that have happened in the last two months. I think about how Rose's and Kurt's lives were far from perfect, but they made their relationship work. They had a beautiful family. I think about how Rose needed more at one point, but as it turned out, everything she needed she had with Kurt, and within herself. I am so lost in thought, the ride goes really quickly. As we pull into the hotel, there is a limo pulling out. The woman in the backseat has a streak of gray in her hair, and she looks at me and smiles. There's something in her clear eyes that startles me. I take a quick breath in, and Lola says, "What is it?"

"Nothing," I say as I watch her disappear down the road. *Was that the psychic?*

I remember what she said when we left each other the first time. *If you need me, I will be there.*

The hair was the same, and there was something in her smile, like she knew I was going to cross her path. Was it her, or am I completely mad, as Lola would say?

"I think I'm seeing things," I say.

When we get into the elevator I allow myself a smile. The couple next to me must think I'm smiling at them, but I'm just elated by how crazy everything is, how unexpected life can be. As if to prove my point, when we get back to our room, Theo is sitting on the floor outside the door, reading a cycling magazine. A T-shirt hugs the contours of his broad chest, and his strong, shaved legs are curled under him.

"Theo?"

He looks scared I might hit him or something. Lola turns back toward the elevator and says, "I'm just going to grab some tea downstairs."

I turn toward Theo, who says, "Liv, Hope told me you came by. I'm so sorry you had to see that. It wasn't . . ."

"It wasn't what?"

"It was a rehearsal. She was my scene partner."

"Really?"

We go inside the room and he says, "You know, we may have gone a little fast. The girl you saw was part of my acting thing, but there *was* someone else. Someone I met up north."

"I knew it."

"I didn't think I'd miss her, but I did, a little. Anyway, I found out she's with someone else now. Besides, it wasn't realistic, being long-distance and all."

"Well, we never said we were boyfriend and girlfriend. I just wish you hadn't acted like we were."

Theo walks over to the window and looks out. "I know. But maybe we can start again? Slowly?"

I think about Blake, his number in my pocket. I remember Lola telling me once that the person you lose your virginity to is usually not the person you end up with. Still, Theo looks pretty adorable in the wash of sunlight filling the room.

"I'm not sure. Maybe," I say, kind of under my breath. Then I decide to change the subject. "Did you get the part?"

"I'm short-listed, whatever that means. I don't think I'm

going to do it, though. It's weird, I'm not desperate like some of the other kids I'm up against. My heart's not totally in it . . . not like when I'm riding."

He brings out a brown paper bag that has a small chocolate cake and a carton of raspberries in it.

"Nice touch with the raspberries," I tell him.

"I'm not all that bad, am I?"

"Jury's out."

He smiles like I'm kidding, but I'm not sure I am. Bell always told me there's a half-truth behind every joke.

We take turns putting on our suits in the bathroom and go down to the beach. The sun is strong, and the sand is almost too hot to walk on. Theo lays out a towel, and we both sit. I show him a picture of my mother, one she gave me. She's standing with the older man who cleans the floors.

"She's beautiful!" he says.

"Well, she definitely has a . . . presence."

"What's with the cane?"

"Mmm. It's complicated. But what isn't? I'm glad I found her. But I had an epiphany, sort of. I realized that sometimes you have to search for something to realize you had it all along."

"That makes sense. Sort of," Theo says.

"It's just—I thought this huge part of my life was missing, but even though I'm so happy I found her, I think I've figured out I don't really need her. The truth is, I've always had everything I need. Maybe that's the secret ingredient—knowing what you have."

Some seagulls swerve over our heads and land near the shore with a flourish.

"Tell me this," I say. "Do you think there's some grand scheme to our lives and we just have to, like, give in to it?"

Theo thinks for a minute, then says, "Something like that."

I tilt my head back. The sky is so bright I feel like someone painted it there—a big unknown, a great escape.

"Let's go," I say.

I jump up and sprint toward the edge of the sea. I gain speed and leap over the first wave, then another. Then I am underwater, holding my breath and kicking fast, with no end in sight. The definition of freedom. What was I waiting for?

I dive a little deeper, and finally come up for air.

ACKNOWLEDGMENTS

To my agent, Mitchell Waters: thank you for going the extra mile in a race I couldn't be running without you.

To my über-editor extraordinaire, Rebecca Short: I thank my lucky stars on a daily basis for having someone as keen and clever as you on my side. You rock.

To my friends who allowed me to shack up and write in their beautiful homes: Bill Candiloros of Ft. Lauderdale, Steve and Chris of Water Island, Elaine and Marsha of Miami, Carole and Mike of Nantucket. (Can you tell I like to write by the ocean?)

To Augusten Burroughs, for making the whole author-photo thing easy and fun, and David Levithan for all that you do for YA authors in the New York City area.

To Chris Carvalho for the lyrics to "Hole in the Sky" and Sharon Foehl for the lyrics to "Similar War."

To Steve Swenson and my daughter, Rowan, for being such bright lights in my life.

Lastly, to my readers: you make it all possible.

ABOUT THE AUTHOR

STEWART LEWIS is a singer-songwriter and radio journalist and is the author of *You Have Seven Messages*. He lives in Washington, D.C. Visit Stewart at stewartlewis.com.